**SPECIAL MESSAGE TO READERS**

**THE ULVERSCROFT FOUNDATION**
**(registered UK charity number 264873)**
was established in 1972 to provide funds for research, diagnosis and treatment of eye diseases. Examples of major projects funded by the Ulverscroft Foundation are:

- The Children's Eye Unit at Moorfields Eye Hospital, London
- The Ulverscroft Children's Eye Unit at Great Ormond Street Hospital for Sick Children
- Funding research into eye diseases and treatment at the Department of Ophthalmology, University of Leicester
- The Ulverscroft Vision Research Group, Institute of Child Health
- Twin operating theatres at the Western Ophthalmic Hospital, London
- The Chair of Ophthalmology at the Royal Australian College of Ophthalmologists

You can help further the work of the Foundation by making a donation or leaving a legacy. Every contribution is gratefully received. If you would like to help support the Foundation or require further information, please contact:

**THE ULVERSCROFT FOUNDATION**
**The Green, Bradgate Road, Anstey**
**Leicester LE7 7FU, England**
**Tel: (0116) 236 4325**
**website: www.ulverscroft-foundation.org.uk**

# CHRISTMAS AT CWTCH COVE

Single mum Carrie has been feeling a bit lost since her daughter headed off to university. She avoids her empty nest by devoting even more time than usual to her cleaning business.

Website developer Ryan lives in a luxury apartment in Bristol, and tells himself all the time that life couldn't be better. The problem is, he feels like something's missing.

When Ryan returns to Cwtch Cove to help his parents with the sale of their house, he bumps into his old friend Carrie. As they get to know each other again, the snow starts falling and the festivities begin . . .

RACHEL GRIFFITHS

# CHRISTMAS AT CWTCH COVE

*Complete and Unabridged*

LINFORD ROMANCE

LINFORD
*Leicester*

First published in Great Britain in 2022

First Linford Edition
published 2025
by arrangement with
LBA Books



*A catalogue record for this book is available
from the British Library.*

ISBN 978–1–4448–5667–5

Published by
Ulverscroft Limited
Anstey, Leicestershire

Printed and bound by CPI Group (UK) Ltd.,
Croydon, CR0 4YY
This book is printed on acid-free paper

MIX
Paper | Supporting responsible forestry
FSC® C013604

# 1

Carrie Baker looked around the clean en-suite bathroom and smiled with pride. The sink and shower cubicle were sparkling, there were fresh bottles of complimentary shampoo, conditioner and shower gel on the shelves and there wasn't a speck of toothpaste or shaving foam on the mirror above the sink.

Back in the bedroom, Levi Watson, one of her team, was cleaning the inside of drawers and cupboards. Levi had been working for her for two years and they'd become good friends in that time. At twenty-two, he was twenty-three years younger than her and could easily have been her son. With his warm nature and witty sense of humour, Levi was good company and he often made Carrie laugh.

'Deary me!' he exclaimed, as he opened the bottom drawer of one of the bedside cabinets. 'Bet they didn't mean to leave this behind.'

'What is it?' Carrie asked, half dreading the answer. Over the years since she'd set up her cleaning business, Dust Busters, she'd seen all sorts. Nothing much surprised her these days.

Levi turned around, his face contorted in a grimace. 'A polaroid photo.'

Carrie giggled. 'One of *those* photos?'

Levi nodded. 'Shall I bin it?'

'The couple who stayed here might want it, so I'll pop it in an envelope and take it to Prime Properties.'

Levi held out the polaroid between finger and thumb and Carrie accepted it in the same way. She glanced at it before sliding it into her apron pocket and shuddered. Why did people take such explicit photos? It was up to the individual, of course, but leaving them lying around afterwards was a bit irresponsible. If it wasn't for her and her team, the next person to stay at the clifftop cottage could see the photo and end up traumatised.

'When you've finished the drawers, we

can make up the bed. I'll go and see how Daisy's getting along downstairs while you check there are no more . . . saucy snapshots anywhere.'

'No problem.' While Levi opened the next drawer, Carrie went down to the kitchen. Daisy was dancing around as she wiped down the fronts of the kitchen cupboards and Carrie knew that she'd have her earphones in. Not wanting to startle Daisy, Carrie went back through the hallway and opened the front door the headed to her van. Once she'd safely deposited the photograph in the plastic box she reserved for such things, she locked the van and was about to return to the cottage, but decided to grab a breath of fresh air instead.

The cottage sat in grounds overlooking Cwtch Cove beach along with several other holiday lets. Prime Properties managed the rental cottages for the owners who made substantial profits from them, especially during the summer months. Winter tended to be a quieter time, but even so, two of the cottages were booked out for late November and all of December, and another over the Christmas holiday, so Carrie and her team had to get the properties ready for the new guests. The first one was arriving tomorrow to stay in Shore House Cottage and the previous guests had only left yesterday, so Carrie, Levi and Daisy had worked all morning. With a business like hers, reputation was incredibly important, and while Prime Properties currently only used Dust Busters in Cwtch Cove, Carrie knew that it might not always be that way. High standards had to be adhered to. A slip could lead to a bad Trip Advisor review or similar and that could lead to Dust Busters losing work, something Carrie couldn't allow to happen.

She gazed out across the beach to the cliffs at the other side. With it being November, the sky was goose grey, the sea dark and choppy, the air sharp with brine and also a hint of engine oil. But even on a day like today, Carrie loved looking at the sea and adored the sense of freedom she felt living in Cwtch Cove. Located about forty minutes west of Tenby on the Pembrokeshire Coast, it was the location that, for her, had always been home. It was where she felt safe and secure, where she spent most of her time and where she wanted to spend the rest of her days. Her life hadn't always worked out the way she'd thought it would but she was happy enough. And she was certainly busy enough.

When she headed back inside the cottage, she found Levi and Daisy in the kitchen together.

'There she is!' Levi said. 'Show Daisy that polaroid.'

'I just put it in *The Box*.'

'*The Box*!' Daisy laughed. 'It must be bad if it's been relegated to *The Box*.'

The fact that Carrie had a box for some of the things they found while cleaning — that she would hand over to Prime Properties — was a source of amusement for Levi and Daisy, and so *The Box* had become an official term.

'It wasn't something I'd want to look

at again,' Carrie said with a shudder.

'I'll have a peak when we go out to the van,' Daisy said with a wink as she adjusted the colourful scarf that held her afro hair back from her forehead.

'I'd spare yourself the shock if I were you,' Levi said. 'My eyes still hurt and I think I'm scarred for life now.'

Carrie smiled at their teasing. She was glad that Levi and Daisy got on because it would have made things difficult if her team members didn't see eye to eye. Daisy had only joined them six months ago. She'd grown up in Birmingham where she'd lived with her parents, had studied sports science at university and become interested in body building. After five years on the body building circuit, she'd quit, although she still worked out regularly. She'd told Carrie that she'd found competing hard because she wasn't naturally competitive and had reached a point in her life when she wanted to settle down not travel constantly. She'd ended up in Cwtch Cove because her aunt owned the caravan park and had invited Daisy to stay in exchange for help around the park. Daisy worked part time with Dust Busters and spent the rest of her time helping her aunt. At thirty-two, she was a whirlwind of energy and Carrie loved having her around.

'Let's get that bed made then, Levi, and we can lock up and head home.'

'Sure thing, boss.'

Upstairs, they spread the crisp white sheet across the bed and stretched it over the corners of the mattress then put on pillow cases and the duvet cover. After Carrie had smoothed out the quilt, she looked up to find Levi grinning at her.

'What?' she asked, stretching out her back. 'Why're you looking at me like that?'

'Just wondering who's going to be renting Shore House next that's all. What if it's a hot single guy?'

'You say that every time and it's usually a couple or a family.'

'But it could be a hot single guy who'll fall madly in love with you.'

'If it is a single man, he could just as

easily fall for you as for me. You're young and handsome, footloose and fancy free.'

Levi gave a small shrug. 'Perhaps. But so are you.'

'Levi,' Carrie laughed, 'I am hardly young or footloose and fancy free.'

'Of course you are.'

'I'm forty-five, a single mother, although my baby girl is miles away at Reading University, and I have a cleaning business and two cats. I don't think I'm exactly a catch, do you?'

'Carrie, you're far too mean to yourself. You're beautiful, independent and successful. You have your own home, your own business and your own teeth.' He winked. 'You're definitely a catch.'

'Hmmm.' Carrie shook her head. She hadn't felt like a catch in a long time. Hadn't given romance a thought in a long time, and right now, she didn't think she had the energy or inclination to consider it. 'There's no one in Cwtch Cove that I find attractive and I doubt anyone here finds me attractive either. That ship has sailed and it left the port a long time ago. I'm too busy, too tired and too old for romance now.' As she said the words, something deep inside her tried to protest so she silenced it quickly.

'I think you're wrong. We have to dream, don't we? And you deserve to be happy just as much as everyone else.'

'I am happy.' Carrie smiled then turned around to check the bedroom one more time. As she went out to the landing, her gaze fell on a framed print on the wall.

'In the end, we only regret the chances we didn't take,' she read the words out loud.

'Exactly.' Levi paused halfway down the stairs to look up at her. 'All I'm saying is that it wouldn't hurt you to take a chance on love if the right man came along.'

'I hear you,' she said, shaking her head. But as she followed Levi downstairs, she bit back the reply, 'And the chances of the right man coming along are slim to none.'

Carrie had been single for the past

fifteen years, since she'd split with her daughter's father, and she couldn't imagine that changing now. She didn't know if she'd even want it to change if she was completely honest. Once bitten, twice shy was what she kept telling herself. She'd been hurt in the past and didn't fancy going through that type of pain again.

* * *

Ryan Davies dropped his washbag into his suitcase then looked up. What else would he need for several weeks at a rental cottage in Cwtch Cove in winter? He'd packed clothes, underwear, pyjamas, trainers, boots, coats, hats and gloves, spare glasses, toiletries and his electric razor. His laptop bag was on the bed along with his laptop, phone, iPad, AirPods and relevant chargers. If he forgot anything, it wouldn't be the end of the world as he could pick up a replacement, but he did need to ensure that he could work while he was away because being self-employed meant that he had to keep his website design business running. He could afford to take a few days off, hell, a few weeks, but he often had clients emailing with questions, so he liked to make himself available to them even if he was meant to be taking a break.

He opened a drawer to grab some more socks and came across what looked like a scrap of crimson silk. He pulled it out and held it up, realising that it was one of his ex-girlfriend's nightdresses. Belinda was an aspiring actress, a beautiful young woman with long blonde hair (some of it extensions), long dark eyelashes (not her own), and a figure that turned heads wherever she went. Ryan had found her attractive, enjoyed her company, but something had been missing. The spark that should have made him keen to see her regularly, made him want to commit to their relationship, made him want to take her home to meet his parents, simply wasn't there. And over the course of six months of dating Belinda, he'd realised that it wasn't there for her either.

Belinda had liked Ryan's money, his apartment and the gym in the basement of the building — complete with sauna and steam room — but she hadn't really liked Ryan that much. And so, when she'd told him she'd got a part as an extra on an action movie being filmed in Dubai, he'd waved her off without a moment's hesitation. They hadn't seen each other since. He dropped the nightdress in the bin, aware that he probably wouldn't get the chance to return it to its owner and he didn't think it was the type of thing you could take to a charity shop.

A whine from the bedroom doorway caught his attention and he looked over to see his French bulldog, Eric, standing there with two of his toys in his mouth.

'Are we packing those, boy?' he asked. Eric ran over to the bed and dropped the toys at Ryan's feet. 'I take it that's a yes.'

He had a separate bag for Eric because some of the toys got a bit smelly with Eric carrying them around in his mouth all the time and Ryan didn't want them making his clothes smelly too. He picked up the rabbit by a soggy ear and the teddy bear with one leg and dropped them into Eric's bag.

Ryan turned back to speak to Eric but the dog was already trotting away again only to return with his blanket. It was a faux fur thing that Ryan's mum had bought for Eric after Ryan first adopted him from a rescue centre in Bristol two years ago. Eric had been taken there after his owner had decided to move to Spain and to leave the dog behind. At a year old, he'd been a timid little thing, frightened of his own shadow, and it had taken time and patience to bring him out of his shell. But now, he was a devoted companion and Ryan took him everywhere. With his fawn fur and big brown eyes, Eric got lots of attention and Ryan admired how the dog had adapted from being afraid of people to being at ease around them. Dogs were amazing creatures and if Ryan had a house and large garden of his own, and not a rented apartment with a small balcony, he'd have adopted more. As it was,

Eric had Ryan all to himself, apart from when Ryan had female company, and that hadn't happened in a while. Any woman who wanted to spend time with Ryan had to be prepared to spend time with Eric too.

Ryan accepted the blanket from Eric then folded it and dropped it into Eric's bag. He smiled because he knew that Eric would want the toys and blanket to sleep tonight, but for now, he'd humour the small dog because Eric was clearly keen to join in. Plus, Ryan wanted to reassure Eric that wherever he went, so did his best friend too.

# 2

'Is that coffee I can smell?' Carrie's sister, Tilly, grinned at her from the doorstep.

'It is. Come on in.' Carrie smiled in return. Tilly sometimes stopped by for coffee before heading to work in Tenby or just for a chat if it was the weekend.

They went through to the open-plan kitchen-diner then Carrie poured coffee from the cafetière into two mugs. She handed Tilly one before taking hers to the L-shaped sofa in front of the bifold doors that overlooked her small but pretty back garden. She sat down and Tilly perched at the end of the sofa, peering at the cushions.

'It's OK, I vacuumed them yesterday.'

'I just don't want my black suit covered in cat hair.'

'Well don't come here in your work clothes then.' Carrie poked out her tongue and Tilly laughed. 'And come to think of it, why are you in your suit on a Saturday?'

Tilly lifted her chin. 'I have a few things to catch up with at the office.'

'Do you lawyers never rest?'

'I do . . . . I just had a lot on last week and I don't want it spilling over into next week.'

'Well try to have the afternoon off at least, won't you?'

'I'll try.' Tilly smiled primly.

'Do you want something to eat?' Carrie was forever trying to feed Tilly, believing that her sister needed to eat more. Tilly had been through a tough few years and Carrie worried about her a lot. With her recent change of hairstyle from long hair to a blonde highlighted pixie cut, her cheekbones were even more accentuated than before.

'I'm fine, thanks. I had an apple.'

'An apple? That's not enough before a morning at work.'

'It's fine. I'll grab something later.'

'Will you?' Carrie watched her sister's face carefully. Tilly was nine years younger than Carrie and she'd always worried about her and felt protective of her. In a lot of ways, she believed she'd been more of a mother figure to Tilly than their own mother had.

'I will. I promise.' Tilly inclined her head then sipped her coffee. 'Mmm. This is good.'

'Only the best coffee will do to start the day.' Carrie raised her mug and sipped it, savouring the rich, caramel flavour.

A meow from the doorway caught her attention. 'Hey Purrito, come here, girl.' The black cat trotted over to her and rubbed herself against Carrie's hand. 'Where's your sister?'

'Still in bed if she has any sense,' Tilly said.

'You're probably right about that.' When Carrie had got up at six a.m., Purrito and Mittens had still been sprawled out on her bed, neither cat showing signs of getting up anytime soon. Carrie wished she could sleep half as well as her cats did. They'd shared her house and bed for the past six years, since she adopted them from a local rescue centre when they were cute little kittens. Purrito was completely black but Mittens was black with white paws, and Purrito had green eyes whereas Mittens' eyes were yellow. Their personalities were very different. Purrito was affectionate; Mittens was more independent, but she loved them both and knew that without their company, her cottage would far too quiet.

Purrito jumped up on the sofa then curled up on her lap so she put her coffee down on the side table and ran her hands over the cat's silky fur.

'Have you heard from Sonia recently?'

'Not for a few days. I had a WhatsApp message on Monday but it was quite brief.'

'Me too. She must be working hard again.'

Carrie fought the urge to roll her eyes. Their mother, Sonia, had left Cwtch Cove five years ago to live in Limone on Lake Garda with her second husband. Sonia had gone out there on holiday with a friend and fallen in love with a handsome, rich Italian. He'd proposed two weeks after they met and Sonia had only come home a handful of times since then, mainly to get some of her things and to sort the sale of the family home. Carrie and her siblings had been concerned that Sonia was rushing into things but their mother had brushed their concerns away. She had always been quite bohemian, seeming to drift through life on a cloud of yoga and incense sticks. And fittingly then, she seemed to float into her second marriage and away from her children as easily as if she was deciding what bread to use for a sandwich. Matteo Romano was a suave, retired businessman with a head of thick salt and pepper hair, twinkling brown eyes and bushy chest hair that showed above his shirt collar. He spoke broken English and smiled a lot. Carrie, her brother, Sean, and Tilly had met him at his villa in Limone, seen for themselves that he was wealthy and not after their mother's money, and accepted that Sonia was happy and would be fine. Matteo seemed particularly enthusiastic about Sonia's art — she'd always been a painter and sculptor — and so she'd progressed from watercolours of the Pembrokeshire coastline to dramatic Italian landscapes and oil paintings featuring lots of lemons.

'It must be hard painting lakes and mountains with a Bellini in your hand, a bowl of fresh olives at your side and an adoring Italian asking if you want a new pair of designer shoes.' Tilly giggled.

'What a life, eh?' Carrie sighed. 'At least she's happy.'

'Exactly.' Tilly drained her coffee. 'And on that note, I should be going or I won't be feeling very happy on Monday when my work is piling up.'

'You work too hard,' Carrie said not for the first time.

'What else would I do to keep busy?' Tilly raised her eyebrows and Carrie winced inwardly. Tilly had separated from her husband two years ago after struggles to conceive naturally followed by several rounds of IVF put strain on their relationship. Tilly and her husband had loved each other but felt they couldn't go on. Carrie suspected that Tilly had instigated the separation because she wanted to free her husband from the marriage so he could try to have a baby with someone else. Tilly would never admit this when Carrie had tried to speak to her about it, other than to say that she wanted him to be happy.

'Are you coming for lunch tomorrow?' Carrie asked.

Tilly stood up and picked at imaginary cat hair on her trousers. 'Try and stop me. Sean and Gwen coming too?'

'Think so.'

'Brilliant. I'll bring dessert.'

'Great.'

Carrie saw her sister to the door then watched as she drove away. Even though she had a daughter of her own now, she'd still worry about Tilly and Sean, still long to see them both happy and content. With their father dead ten years and their mother living abroad, Carrie felt responsible for her siblings, her niece

Gwen too, and she did what she could to take care of them all.

Turning, she saw Mittens making her way down the stairs. Time to make the cats their breakfast then get some chores done. Shore House Cottage was on her mind, as if she'd forgotten to do something when she was there yesterday. It was probably something minor, because Carrie rarely forgot anything on her mental checklist, but hopefully the answer would come to her soon.

* * *

Ryan parked the car outside his parents' home and got out. He stretched his legs then opened the back door. Eric peered up at him sleepily.

'We're here!' Ryan said, injecting some enthusiasm into his tone to hopefully wake Eric up. He leant into the car and unclipped the dog's safety harness then lifted him out of the car and set him on the pavement. Eric had a good shake then went to the nearest tree and cocked his back leg. 'Good boy.'

The journey from Bristol to Cwtch Cove had taken three hours. He'd stopped twice to let Eric stretch his legs and have a wee and to get something to eat, but apart from that, the drive had been quite straightforward.

He closed the car door and surveyed the house he'd grown up in. He'd been back over the years and his parents had come to stay with him, but this time was different. His parents had sold their home and were moving into a retirement flat in a new complex that had been built on the outskirts of the village. Both in their seventies, they were still healthy but finding the house a bit big for their needs, and so they'd decided to sell up and move into a ground floor flat at the complex. Ryan felt a bit guilty because if he lived closer, he thought that they might have felt more comfortable staying in their own home, but the retirement flat came with warden support and so offered them a sense of security. It would also be easier to keep clean and warm, his mother had told him on the phone, and after he'd seen the photographs, he had to agree. It would be perfect for their changing needs.

He walked up the driveway and the front door swung open. Eric raced on ahead and straight towards Ryan's mum, Blodwen, who bent over to make a fuss of the dog. Ryan waited until Eric had his fill of belly rubs then he hugged his mother himself.

'Darling! So happy to see you.'

'Happy to see you too, Mum,' he said, breathing in her familiar floral perfume, trying not to worry that she felt smaller in his arms, as if she'd shrunk since he'd last seen her.

'Your dad's inside labelling boxes.'

'He'll be enjoying that then.' Ryan laughed. His dad did like organising things.

'Oh yes. And he's loved clearing things out. Every time I protest he says, 'Blodwen! We can't take it all with us.' Then he throws something out or into the charity box. There's a pile of your old things in your room so you might want to look through it before the skip comes.'

'No problem.' Ryan swallowed a sigh. He was tired after the journey and wanted a cuppa and something to eat, as well as to take his things up to the rental cottage, but for now, it seemed, his parents had plans for him.

He followed his mum and Eric inside, hoping he'd at least get a cup of tea before they asked him to start looking through his old belongings.

# 3

'Hello Aunty Carrie!' Six-year-old Gwen flung herself at Carrie as soon as she opened the door.

Carrie scooped her up and hugged her tight. 'Hello, my cherub.'

'Dinner smells delicious.' Gwen sniffed loudly. 'My tummy's so empty it thinks my head's fallen off.'

Carrie saw her brother shaking his head and smiling behind Gwen.

'Your tummy thinks your head has fallen off. My goodness! We can't have that now, can we?' Carrie laughed as she carried Gwen through to the kitchen.

'I don't know where she gets some of the things she says.' Sean placed a bottle of wine and a box of chocolates on the kitchen table. 'These are for you, by the way.'

Carrie set Gwen down on the sofa. 'Thanks, baby brother.'

'Daddy's not a baby!' Gwen giggled.

'He's far too big and hairy to be a baby.'

'He'll always be a baby to me.' Carrie winked at her niece and Gwen rolled about on the sofa giggling as if it was the funniest thing she'd ever heard.

'Where are the cats?' Gwen asked once she'd composed herself.

'I think they're upstairs.'

'Can I go and see them?'

'Please,' Sean said.

'Please?' Gwen smiled at Carrie.

'Of course you can.'

'Yay!' Gwen raced up the stairs leaving Carrie checking out the wine Sean had brought.

'Thanks for this. I'll pop it in the fridge. Do you want a glass of wine now or a soft drink?'

'I'll have a glass of wine. I'm off duty today so I'd just as well relax a bit.'

'Glad to hear it. You work too hard.'

'I'm a single parent. I have to provide.'

Carrie nodded sadly. Sean's wife, Lara, had passed away four years earlier following a late diagnosis of ovarian cancer. She'd been Sean's high school sweetheart and they'd both been science and animal mad, had gone to university together to study veterinary science and then set up their own practice in the village after graduating. They'd had a wonderful wedding, worked hard and been very happy. Carrie had wondered if they would have a family because they'd seemed so content as they were, but then, when they were both thirty-one, they announced that they were three months pregnant, and six months later, Gwen was born. When Gwen was eighteen months old, Lara thought the pains she was having were linked to the endometriosis she'd always suffered from, but tests showed otherwise and by then the cancer was advanced. And just like that, one summer's day, she was gone.

Carrie blinked hard. She'd loved Lara and was heartbroken seeing her slip away, but for Sean, it had been devastating. His grief was overwhelming, and Carrie had worried that he wouldn't make it through. But with Gwen needing him, his two sisters supporting him and his veterinary practice, somehow he managed it. Carrie knew he wasn't the same man and probably never would be; grief could do that to a person, but he was a good father, a brilliant vet and a loving brother. Sean simply got on with things. What else could he do? Carrie knew what it was like to cope with pain and loss, if not the same kind as Sean's, and she also knew that a person had two choices — carry on or give up. When there were people reliant upon you, especially children, you simply had to carry on.

'I know, lovely,' Carrie said, squeezing Sean's arm. 'And you love your job.'

He smiled. 'Working with animals is the best.'

'I'm glad you feel that way. Right . . . I'll get that wine.'

Carrie opened the fridge and put the wine from Sean inside then got a cold bottle out. After she'd poured some into glasses, she gestured at the sofa.

'Shall we have a sit down while the veg cooks?'

They'd just sat down when there was a loud bang from overhead.

'Shit! What was that?' Sean jumped up, spilling some of his wine over his jeans. 'Gwen? You OK?' he shouted.

No reply.

Sean put his wine down and hurried from the kitchen and Carrie followed. As she ran up the stairs, pictures of Gwen lying on the bedroom floor hurt rushed through her mind and cold fear gripped her heart. Gwen was only six. She was so young, so small and so precious.

'Bloody hell, Gwen!' Sean was standing in Carrie's bedroom doorway shaking his head. 'Are you all right?'

'I'm fine, Daddy.'

Carrie couldn't see her niece but hearing her reply made her clutch her chest in relief. Gwen was fine. Everything was fine. She bent over to catch her breath then went to Sean's side and peered past him into the bedroom.

'What happened?' she asked.

'I was trying to cuddle Mittens but she didn't want to cuddle me and she jumped up there.' Gwen pointed at the top of the wardrobe where Mittens sat, eyes wide, glaring down at them. 'And she knocked your box off the top.'

Carrie's gaze moved to the floor where a shoebox lay, lid off, contents spilling over the floorboards. 'Well as long as you're OK,' she said. She crossed the room and picked up the box then reached for the photographs and other things that had fallen out. As she did so, she glanced at the top photo and her heart skipped a beat. It was of her when she was about seventeen. She was standing between two male friends, one of whom she hadn't seen in ages — Ryan Davies — and the other — Grant — who'd become her partner.

'Who are those boys?' Gwen asked as she took the photo from Carrie.

'Oh . . . just some friends I went to school with,' Carrie said. 'That one there is Amy's dad.' Gwen didn't know Grant because they'd split up long before she'd come along.

'Ha! Ha! Look at your hair, Aunty

Carrie.'

'It's quite a mop,' Sean said as he looked at the photo.

'Shut up, you two! Perms and big hair were fashionable back then.'

'Wasn't that your glam rock phase?' Sean asked nudging Carrie.

'Something like that.' She rolled her eyes at him then put the photo back in the box. 'Where's Purrito?' she asked, realising that she hadn't seen her other cat.

'There.' Gwen pointed at the bed where she'd lined up some of Amy's old dolls and teddy bears. At the centre of them was Purrito, blinking at Carrie, looking completely unfazed by it all.

'What's she wearing?' Sean approached the bed.

'A dress off Amy's old dolly.'

'Nice.' Sean gave a nod of approval then turned to Carrie. She shrugged. If Purrito was happy to be dressed up, then who was she to intervene?

'Perhaps we should go downstairs and leave Mittens to come down when she's ready,' Carrie said, glancing at the cat on top of the wardrobe. It seemed that Mittens had no intention of being dressed up like her sister.

'Mittens clearly has her own ideas about style,' Sean muttered to Carrie.

'It looks that way.' Carrie shook her head.

'OK. Come on then, Purrito.' Gwen went to the bed and reached for Purrito. The cat allowed Gwen to pick her up and carry her like a baby. 'Let's go downstairs and have some chicken, shall we?'

Purrito meowed in response and Carrie smiled at Sean.

'I'll just check that Mittens is OK,' he said. 'I hate the thought of her being scared.'

'Good idea,' Carrie said as she followed Gwen from the room. Sean would want to check that Mittens wasn't scared, but Carrie suspected he also needed a moment to calm himself. Losing Lara had left him terrified of losing Gwen and of Gwen being hurt in any way, so he faced a daily battle with his urge to wrap her up in cotton wool. Carrie and Tilly both tried to reassure him constantly, but ultimately it was something he had to deal with, and Carrie thought he was doing an excellent job.

* * *

'Thanks for taking us out to lunch,' Ryan's mum patted her belly. 'I'm stuffed but it was absolutely delicious, wasn't it, Griffin?'

'Bit of a drive just for lunch though, Blodwen,' his dad said with a wink. He was very concerned about using fuel because of the constant price hikes and liked to share his opinion on it every chance he got. Ryan completely understood where he was coming from but had wanted to take his parents out and treat them.

'My pleasure,' Ryan replied. 'I should do it more often. I'll try to while I'm here.' The country pub he'd brought them to had excellent reviews that claimed the food was top quality. They hadn't been wrong.

On the chair next to him, Eric peered at the table, scanning the plates to check for scraps. His mum had sneaked the dog chicken, carrots and peas throughout dinner and Eric had been delighted. He knew that he had his grandmother wrapped around his paw and Ryan was a bit concerned that Eric would get fat if he spent too much time with Blodwen and Griffin.

'My pots and pans are all packed so I can't cook a thing until we move,' his mother said, holding up her hands.

'Any excuse,' his dad said, chuckling.

'Darling, you're quite capable of cooking too, you know.' Ryan's mother poked her tongue out at his father and Ryan shook his head. Who should cook was an age old debate in his parents' home but it always ended up with them all laughing. His father had worked as a fisherman while his mother had stayed home to raise him and look after the house, but even so, at weekends his father had taken over the kitchen and treated them all to pancake breakfasts, spicy chicken curry and large Sunday dinners with amazing roast potatoes. And since he'd retired, Ryan knew his father had pulled his weight around the house. Whenever he Facetimed them, he often found them cooking up a storm in the kitchen together, doing jigsaws or gardening. They were a happy couple, good friends and enjoyed their time together. Ryan had always thought he'd end up with a partner like that but somehow, it hadn't happened. He'd come to the conclusion that not everyone was lucky enough to meet their soulmate.

'Right, I'm going to powder my nose,' his mother said, pushing her chair back. As she stood up, she winced.

'What's wrong?' he asked, jumping up.

'Nothing, my darling. Just a touch of stiffness in my joints. Happens as you get older.'

His mother smiled but he could see something in her eyes that looked a lot like pain. As she walked away from the table, he watched her carefully. She seemed thinner than she had been when he'd last visited, less agile, as if time really was taking its toll. She was only seventy though. Surely that was still young? People lived into their nineties and beyond these days.

'She's OK, you know,' his father said and Ryan looked at him.

'Of course,' he said, though he had a sinking feeling in his stomach. He'd lived away for years and take it for granted that his parents were fine. They'd always been so strong and independent. They'd openly expressed their worries about him but he hadn't thought he needed to worry about them. Only now . . . seeing them both, he couldn't deny that they were getting older. Had it happened suddenly or had he ignored the signs before because he'd been so wrapped up in his own life? Or, hadn't he wanted to see it, and now, because there was change on the horizon — with them moving out of their home — he couldn't ignore the fact that they were ageing any longer?

His dad reached out and lifted Eric onto his lap and stroked the dog's small head. Eric closed his eyes, happy to bask in the attention. With Ryan being an only child and him never having children, Eric was the only grandchild his parents seemed likely to get. They'd never complained about that fact and had only asked him if there was someone special on a handful of occasions. They'd been wonderful parents, content to let Ryan live his life, there for him when he needed them, and giving him space when he wanted to spread his wings. Sometimes though, he felt a pang that they'd never have a grandchild of their own and sad that he'd never given them that joy. But he was forty-five now and thought it was getting more and more unlikely to happen. Thankfully, though, Eric seemed to be doing a good job of being a substitute grandchild.

Perhaps it was time for Ryan to consider getting him a canine sibling. It was something he'd considered before but he'd been waiting for the right time. He'd give it some more thought while he was in Cwtch Cove. He felt sure Eric would be happy having a friend and his parents would be delighted having another dog around.

* * *

'What's for dessert, Aunty Carrie?' Gwen asked while patting Carrie's hand. The little girl had insisted on sitting next to Carrie at the table and throughout dinner she'd repeatedly patted Carrie's hand, arm and leg to get her attention. It seemed to be a new habit of hers and Carrie found it very cute but suspected that living with it long-term might prove challenging.

'Gwen . . . You just ate enough chicken dinner to fuel an army.' Sean raised his sandy eyebrows at his daughter and she grinned at him.

'I like Aunty Carrie's Sunday dinner. It's the best.'

Sean looked taken aback. 'What? Better than mine?'

‘Hmmmm.’ Gwen pouted and tugged at one of her blonde bunches. ‘A tiny bit, Daddy.’

‘Well!’ Sean shook his head. ‘I’ll have to find out what makes Aunty Carrie’s cooking better than mine, won’t I?’

‘I’m teasing you, Daddy. Yours is just as good.’ Gwen turned to Carrie and blinked at her three times then she leant closer to Carrie and whispered. ‘Did you see me winking at you?’

‘Winking?’ Carrie paused. ‘Do you mean blinking?’

‘No, silly, winking. It means that I’m not telling Daddy the truth. I like his dinners but yours are better. Daddy does the broccoli too crunchy and the carrots aren’t buttery.’

‘I see,’ Carrie whispered back. ‘He tries hard though.’

‘He does, bless him.’ Gwen gave a solemn nod and Carrie had to stifle laughter. ‘Excuse me please because now I need a poo.’

Gwen slid off her chair and headed to the downstairs cloakroom leaving the adults grinning at one another.

'So she can wink now then?' Carrie asked. 'With two eyes.'

'I have tried to explain how it works but it's so cute when she does it that I can't ruin it for her.'

'She's just adorable,' Tilly said. 'I love that she tells the truth. You are a good cook, Sean, but Carrie is better.'

'Thanks, sis. Same to you.' Sean blinked at Tilly three times and she laughed.

'Well that was a good poo,' Gwen said as she returned to the table.

'Gwen, you don't have to share that information.' Sean helped Gwen get up onto the chair.

'Why not? I feel better now and made room for dessert.' Gwen's blue eyes were wide as she gazed at her dad. 'That's good to share, right, Daddy?'

'I guess so.' Sean started to clear the table. 'Thanks for dinner, Carrie, it was delicious.'

'My pleasure. OK then.' Carrie got up and went to the fridge. 'For dessert you can have some of this wonderful looking strawberry trifle that Aunty Tilly kindly brought or there's chocolate ice cream in the freezer.'

She turned and waited while her niece, brother and sister made up their minds.

'Aunty Carrie?' Gwen scratched her chin as if deep in thought. 'Could I possibly have both, please?'

'You most certainly can. Anyone else?'

Sean and Tilly looked at each other and nodded. 'Yes, please!'

'Coming right up.' Carrie got the trifle from the fridge and the ice cream from the freezer then took them to the table while Sean set four bowls out.

Carrie missed her daughter, Amy, but knew she was lucky to have her siblings and niece living nearby. Even if her niece did scare one of her one cats and dress the other one up like a doll.

# 4

Carrie woke the next day with a jolt. She always woke early but this morning, something had snapped her into alertness. She lay there for a moment to try to work out if it had been a dream that had made her stir. If she had something on her mind or had forgotten to do a job, this could happen. She thought about yesterday when her family had come for dinner. Mittens had stayed upstairs until after they'd eaten lunch but then the aroma of chicken had proved too much and she'd come down to wind herself around Carrie's legs until Carrie gave in and fed her some. It had been a very enjoyable afternoon, and Sean, Gwen and Tilly had stayed until late, wrapping up in hats, scarves, gloves and warm coats to walk home. With it being November, it got dark early, so when they'd left the sky had been a black canvas dotted with silver pinpricks and the air crisp and icy.

Later on, the cats had been reluctant to go out to do their business before bed but Carrie had waited on the doorstep for them and then the three of them had headed up to bed to snuggle under the duvet.

Suddenly, it hit Carrie like a bucket of cold water.

'Oh no!' She slapped her forehead. 'Towels!'

She'd forgotten to take more towels to Shore House Cottage before the guest got there. She was certain there were hand towels there but no bath sheets. She'd have to deliver some first thing this morning and apologise profusely because the last thing she wanted was to get a bad review. Perhaps she'd be lucky and the guests wouldn't have showered since they arrived — doubtful seeing as how that was two days ago — or perhaps they were really tiny and hand towels would be fine.

'Who am I trying to kid?' she asked as she pushed the duvet aside and got out of bed. 'Time to get going, Carrie.'

* * *

Fresh out of the shower, Ryan reached for a towel and groaned. He'd meant to contact the rental company about this the previous day but had forgotten. When he'd arrived on Saturday, there had been no proper towels in the cottage. He hadn't thought to bring any because they'd been listed as items provided with the rental information. He'd showered that first evening and kind of drip dried, then yesterday he'd used a hand towel and it looked like he'd have to do the same this morning. He used one to dry his head and shoulders then another to dry the rest of him.

Hearing a noise, he did his best to wrap one of the towels around his waist, grabbed his glasses from the side of the bath and trotted down the stairs, wondering if Eric was scratching at the door to go out. He froze. There was a glass panel in the front door and Eric was in front of it growling. The other side of it was a woman in a padded coat and woolly hat that pulled down to her eyes as if it was too big for her, peering through the glass. Directly at him.

He couldn't exactly run back upstairs because she'd seen him so he'd have to grin and bear it. Holding the towel with one hand, he opened the door with the other and ushered Eric back from the door with his left leg.

'Sit there,' he said to Eric then turned to the woman on the doorstep.

'Oh! Hello!' she said with a wave, averting her eyes. She was holding what looked like a pile of towels. 'I meant to leave these here on Friday when I cleaned. I'm dreadfully sorry. It's a mistake I wouldn't normally make and I don't know how it happened. But it looks like you need them . . . so here you go.'

She held out the towels while still trying not to look at him, and Ryan reached for them with his free hand just as Eric leapt towards the door. She went to pass the towels to him just as he realised he'd have to stop Eric jumping on her, so the towels landed on the dog who yelped with surprise. Ryan scooped the towels aside, but Eric was furious and he showed it by grabbing the hem of the towel around Ryan's waist and tugging at it.

In horror, Ryan tried to hold the towel, but Eric growled playfully and gave it an almighty tug then ran away with it, leaving Ryan with just his hands to hide himself.

He turned to the woman on the doorstep who was no longer looking away but staring at his naked body in shock.

And it hit him as he recognised the face underneath the hat.

This wasn't a stranger.

It was Carrie.

* * *

'Oh my god! I'm so sorry! Is he all right?' Carrie asked, her eyes flickering to the doorway Eric had run through and back to Ryan. 'Are *you* all right?'

She tried to keep her eyes up but he was naked, trying to cover himself with his hands and it was really hard not to look elsewhere. Goosebumps had appeared as the cold morning air met his skin; some patches still glistened with water. She reached for one of the larger towels on the floor, trying not to notice the scent of spicey shower gel, the breadth of his shoulders, the dark hair on his toned chest and the line that led down to his navel and beyond. But her eyes wouldn't behave themselves and they seemed intent on devouring the sight of him.

'Here, take this to cover your pen . . . I mean . . . to cover up.' She held out the towel and he looked down at his hands then back at her. 'I won't look,' she said, placing a hand over her eyes.

'It's OK, now,' he said.

She lowered her hand to find that he'd wrapped the large bath sheet around his middle. His torso was still exposed though, and something rushed through Carrie, a strange kind of heat that made her heart race and her core flutter. It had been a very long time since she'd seen a man almost naked and just as long since she'd been this close to a man wearing only a towel. It had been an incredibly long time since she'd felt like this.

What was this strange but not at all horrid feeling?

A flush rushed to her cheeks and she tried to drag her gaze away but he was like a feast and she was suddenly starving. This man could give Poldark a run for his money!

'Carrie?' he said, and she gasped as she met his eyes.

'Oh . . . It's you! But I haven't seen you in . . . a lifetime. And you look quite different you know?' Her voice rose, revealing her surprise.

'Yes, it's me. And ditto.'

'Ryan?' she asked, needing it confirmed. How had she not recognised him? She'd been worrying about facing a bad review, yes, and the repercussions of that in terms of her contract with Prime Properties, yes. She'd been distracted by his body, yes. But she'd known Ryan well. Albeit a long time ago.

This Ryan, though, was very different. The Ryan she'd known had been . . . younger, slimmer, less . . . broad. 'You're a man.'

He stared at her, his dark eyes behind black framed glasses seeming to see down to the bottom of her soul and then, his lips curved upwards and he laughed.

'I guess I am.'

'I'm sorry. I meant that . . . uh . . . You're all grown up.'

'It seems that way. Being forty-five will do that to you.'

'You look . . . different . . . but the same.' She reached up and tugged the woolly hat from her head, feeling like she might spontaneously combust if she didn't.

'You look well, Carrie.'

'Thanks.' She tried to swallow but her mouth was dry. 'I didn't know you were in the village.'

'I've come to help Mum and Dad move. They've sold their house and they're moving into the new complex.'

'Oh. Right. It is an amazing place. I

went to have a look at it because they want to hire a cleaning business to contract. It's quite a big place though and my team is small. Just the three of us.' *Don't look at his chest!* 'So . . . we uhhh . . . We do have quite a lot of work anyway. That's what I was doing here. I have a cleaning business and we do the cottages, caravan park and some other residences.' *Stop thinking about resting your head on his shoulder!*

'You have your own business? That's great.' He smiled. 'So do I.'

'What do you do?' *Oh dear lord*, he's so hot!

'I'm a front-line developer.'

She frowned. *What on earth does that mean?*

'Basically, I design websites. I do all the stuff that visitors see.'

'Oh?' Carrie nodded. 'I don't have a website but I suppose I should get one. Thing is . . . I only work locally and it's still a lot to do with word of mouth so I'm not sure that a website would be useful, really, but —' *Now you're babbling!*

'It might be if you decided to expand your business. You could get seen then and perhaps get contracts in other villages, towns and possibly cities.'

'Yes. I guess I could.' The idea seemed daunting to Carrie. She was proud of her business but hadn't thought about it being bigger. She was happy with the way things were but could understand why — to someone like Ryan, who'd left Cwtch Cove in his teens — it would seem unambitious. What must he think of her? A big shot IT guy coming back here to find her basically unchanged, still living in the village and doing the same things she'd always done?

'Anyway . . . I'd probably better go and get dressed,' he said.

'Yes. That's a good idea. You'll catch a cold standing on the doorstep naked. I mean . . . almost naked.'

She was about to say goodbye when the tiny French bulldog reappeared, glanced at her then grabbed hold of Ryan's new towel and started tugging at it while growling.

'Bloody hell, Eric! Are you serious?' Ryan held the towel with both hands, laughter in his voice. 'He does this sometimes. Thinks tug of war is a great game.'

'He's very cute.' Carrie thought the little dog was adorable, almost as lovely as his owner.

'Eric! Let go!'

Eric growled. Ryan wrestled with the towel. Carrie tried not to stare.

'I'm going to leave you to it,' Carrie said. 'It was great seeing you again. Perhaps I'll see more of you while you're here.' She winced. 'I mean . . . not more of you as in when your towel dropped but more of you as in . . . Oh dear. I'm going to go. Bye!'

Ryan waved a hand and she headed back to her van, mortification seeping through her. Why had she been such an idiot? Babbled like an awkward teenaged girl? She was a grown woman with an adult daughter and she'd just acted like an embarrassed fool. Worse! A fool with an instant crush on a handsome man. So much for cool and calm in the way she'd imagined she'd act if she ever bumped into Ryan again. Not that she'd thought about him that much, really, but now and then, when she saw posts on Facebook from people they'd gone to school with, she'd wondered where Ryan was, what he was doing, if he was happily married with children of his own.

If he ever thought about her and how close they'd once been.

She realised she was just as ignorant to the answers to those questions as she had been for years. The only thing she did know now was that Ryan had aged like a fine wine. He'd always been attractive, but now, he was drop dead gorgeous.

Looking down at her puffy coat with her apron sticking out from underneath it, catching sight of her messy hair in the rear-view mirror, Carrie had to accept that while Ryan had aged well; she had not. He must've thought she was a right mess.

She pushed her hair back, tugged

her hat back on and started the engine. Never mind, eh, her dating days were long gone. Ryan probably had some sexy model type wife or partner, and if they had children, they were likely just as perfect and adorable. And that was how it should be.

She turned the radio on loud and drove away, trying to focus on today's schedule and what she'd make for dinner. Trying not to think about Ryan and the unfamiliar feelings that had temporarily reared their heads when she'd seen him.

Once upon a time, she hadn't taken a chance and asked him out as she'd wanted to, and she had only herself to blame.

* * *

Ryan stood in the hallway for a while after Carrie had gone. He was in shock for more than one reason. Firstly, he was horribly embarrassed because Carrie had seen him naked. *Bloody Eric grabbing at the tiny towel and running off with it!* Secondly, he was gobsmacked by how beautiful she still was. In fact, she was even more beautiful than he remembered. She'd been stunning as a young woman but now, it was like she'd grown into herself, blossomed and reached her potential.

His cheeks flushed as he thought about what she'd seen, about how her eyes had roamed over his body as if she too was in shock. Probably was after seeing his . . . everything he had on display.

He was interested to find out that she had a cleaning business of her own. She'd always seemed brave and independent, like she'd go after what she wanted. Before he went away to university, he'd been quite close to Carrie and Grant Jones, and at one point, when Grant had gone away on a boys' holiday, Ryan and Carrie had spent some time alone. He'd been trying to summon the courage to ask her out but he'd lacked confidence, wondered if she saw him as the geeky friend. So he hadn't done it, Grant had returned tanned and confident as ever and then it had been time for Ryan to head to university in Bath. But then Carrie and Grant got together while Ryan was away and Grant had seemed, to Ryan, a bit possessive of Carrie. During the holidays, when Ryan had come home, it seemed like Carrie was keen to keep Grant happy and like she'd changed. She spent most of her time with Grant and rarely seemed to go out with her friends anymore. Of course, people often did change when they fell in love, but Ryan had thought Carrie changed a lot. Over the course of his degree, his friendship with Grant and Carrie changed dramatically, to the point where they no longer spent time together. When Ryan decided to move away from Cwtch Cove after university, he only said a very brief goodbye to his old friends.

Was she still with Grant? Did they have a family, a home and a happy life together? Ryan hoped so for Carrie's sake because she deserved to be happy and fulfilled. Ryan had made a point of not asking his parents about Carrie or Grant and over the years they'd stopped sharing news about them. It was the way things went as time passed. And even though he worked as a web designer, Ryan didn't have a personal Facebook. He thought of social media as a bit of a rabbit hole, and he was far too busy to start looking people up to find out what they were doing now. He preferred to live in the present and to be present, for as much time as he could be anyway.

However, he'd seen the name on Carrie's van — Dust Busters — so once he'd got dressed, he'd Google it and find out a bit more about her. Mainly so that if he bumped into her again, he'd have something to talk to her about. Grant too, if he saw his old friend.

'Eric?' Ryan peered into the lounge and sure enough, Eric was in there lying on the hand towel, and if he hadn't known better, Ryan could have sworn the dog was grinning at him. 'That wasn't funny, Eric. It wasn't funny at all.'

However, as he turned to head upstairs, he found himself grinning as he recalled the expression of surprise on Carrie's face. And what a beautiful face it was.

# 5

'It's a month today,' Gwen said as she licked the spoon she'd just stirred her hot chocolate with.

'What is?' Carrie asked, looking up from her phone.

'Christmas Day, silly.' Gwen rolled her eyes.

'Gwen! That's very rude.' Sean shook his head.

'Sorry.' Gwen sighed. 'I'm just very excited, Daddy, and you know how I get when I'm excited.'

'Rude?'

'No, Daddy . . . I get all . . . I don't know . . . like . . . discombobulated.'

Carrie met Sean's eyes over the café table.

'Where did you learn that word?' Sean asked.

'At school. We have word of the week, remember?' Gwen raised her blonde eyebrows.

‘Oh yes. I remember. I’m not quite sure that you mean discombobulated in this context, but I think I know what you’re trying to say.’

‘It’s a good word though,’ Carrie said, stroking Gwen’s blonde curls. ‘A very big word for such a little girl.’

‘It is indeed. Well done, Gwen.’ Sean mouthed *thanks* at Carrie. Sometimes he was so concerned about being a good dad, about educating Gwen correctly, that he forgot about letting some things go. Carrie would never dream of criticising him because he was an amazing dad, but she knew he’d appreciate the gentle reminder here.

‘Thank you, Daddy. I’m going to go to the toilet now because I feel all . . . discombobulated.’ Gwen got down from the table then held up a hand. ‘No need to come with me. The toilet is only through that door and I can manage to have a wee by myself.’

‘Sure. I know that.’ Sean nodded and Carrie sipped her coffee to hide her laughter. When Gwen had gone, Sean said, 'She'll use discombobulated in every situation now.'

'She's adorable so who cares? Amy was exactly the same.' Carrie touched her phone where it lay on the table as she thought about the message she'd just read from her daughter.

'You OK?' Sean asked. 'Anything to worry about?'

'No. It's fine. Well . . . actually . . . I had a text from Amy to give me advance notice that she won't be home for Christmas.'

'Oh?' Sean knitted his brows. 'How come?'

'She's going to spend it with her boyfriend in Reading.'

'Her boyfriend?'

'I didn't know she was seeing anyone either.' Carrie gave a small shrug. 'It's OK though. I mean . . . I knew this would happen at some point. I just wasn't expecting it yet. Although she is twenty now so she was going to get serious with someone sooner or later.' Carrie didn't add that she was two years younger than

Amy when she got together with Grant. How do you feel about that?' Sean asked, his bright blue eyes fixed on Carrie's face.

Carrie inhaled slowly, letting the news sink in properly. After twelve years with Grant, she'd learnt a long time ago not to react, to take her time to digest things before sharing her feelings.

'I'm all right. I'm happy for her. I kind of wish she'd phoned to tell me but I suspect she was nervous about it. You know how Amy is . . . caring and compassionate. She'd just be worried about letting me down or something.' Carrie sipped her coffee. 'And she hasn't! Not at all. I'm old enough to spend Christmas alone.'

'Alone?' Sean laughed. 'When do you ever spend it alone?'

Carrie smiled. 'I know, I know. I'm very lucky I get to spend it with you, Gwen and Tilly, but I'm guessing Amy's thinking about me being on my own over the holidays. Telling me by text is her way of preparing me, I suppose, so when we chat she'll know that I've been forewarned. But it's really not a problem. I mean . . . I'd like to meet the young man who's captured my baby girl's heart but they're young and in love and probably need some time alone. Apparently he's studying pharmacology too, so they'll be able to study together. She does have exams in January so staying in Reading makes a lot of sense, really.'

'It's OK to feel sad about this, you know.' Sean reached for her hand and squeezed it.

'I know.' Carrie swallowed hard. She would not get upset about this. Children grew up and left home, built their own lives. It was a good thing and the fact that Amy felt happy to go to university in Reading and to live so far away from where she'd grown up just showed that Carrie — and Grant to a certain extent — had done a good job. They'd raised a strong, independent young woman who wasn't afraid to head out into the world alone.

*Unlike me . . .*

At Amy's age she'd been afraid to go too far. Her parents hadn't been horrible, but they had been very different. Her father was a quiet, serious accountant who liked his routines; her mother was a free spirit who liked to please herself first and foremost, and whose family were, often, an afterthought. When Carrie's father had died ten years ago from a sudden heart attack, Carrie and her siblings had been shocked and bereft. Their father had been the rock that the family was built upon and their mother seemed to become even more eccentric overnight. It was as if Roger Baker had been her anchor and once he was gone, she was filled with a restless energy that made her long to travel. It had taken her five years to move away to Italy, and her three children had been adults for some time by then, but there were times when Carrie would have appreciated having a mother who was around, who was there for her on occasion. Instead, Carrie had taken over as the maternal figure of the family and she strove to be there for Sean and Tilly, as well as for Amy and Gwen. 'And Amy has given me plenty of notice so everything will be fine.'

Sean knitted his brows. 'Gwen's taking a while.'

'She is. I'll go and check on her.' Carrie got up and went to the door at the rear of the café that led to a small corridor and three separate toilets. She knocked on the door labelled Ladies and waited. Nothing. She knocked again. 'Gwen?'

'Yes!'

'Are you all right?'

'Yes!'

'What's taking you so long?'

'I'm making myself look pretty.'

'Oh . . . OK. Well you've been in there for a while so do you want to come out now? Your hot chocolate will get cold.'

'Hang on!'

Carrie waited outside the door and when it opened she couldn't suppress her gasp of surprise.

'I look good, right?' Gwen grinned up at her and Carrie couldn't do anything other than nod. 'I'm not discombobulated anymore.'

Gwen slid her hand through Carrie's and they went back to the table.

Sean looked up and his eyes widened. 'What the hell?'

'Daddy, don't swear, it's rude.' Gwen got up on her chair and reached for her hot chocolate.

'Gwen?' Sean stared at his daughter. 'What happened to your face?'

'Isn't it great?' Gwen patted her cheeks. 'I put some lipstick on.'

'I can see that.' Sean looked shocked and laughter bubbled inside Carrie. It had been a busy day and she'd come here to meet Sean and Gwen after school, expecting to hear about their days over a quiet drink. Sean had an early finish on Fridays so he could collect Gwen from school. The rest of the time, she was collected by a childminder who had a daughter the same age as Gwen. Fridays had become something to look forward to for Carrie because she got this special time with her brother and niece. Gwen was such a character and she always had an amusing anecdote or fact or word of the week for them, but today she had surpassed herself with a makeover. 'I've never worn lipstick myself, Gwen, but aren't you supposed to put it on your lips?'

'It is on my lips,' Gwen said.

'And around them,' Sean replied. 'As well as on your cheeks.'

'Oh yes, I saw that on YouTube. You can entrance your cheekbones with some colour and careful shading.' Gwen blinked at her father then turned to Carrie. 'You know, Aunty Carrie, you could benefit from entrancing your cheekbones.'

'Is that right?' Carrie raised her eyebrows. '*Entrancing* my cheekbones?'

'Gwen . . . I think you mean enhancing. Also . . . I suspect I'm going to regret asking this but where did you get the lipstick?' Sean was folding and unfolding a napkin as he spoke to his daughter.

'I found it by the mirror.'

'Oh god! So that belongs to someone else?' Sean grimaced. 'It could be anyone's. You could . . . catch something from it or . . .'

'It might be a good idea to wash it off,' Carrie said. 'Just in case the person who it belongs to has a . . . a cold or something.'

'I think it might be a bit late for that, don't you, Aunty Carrie?' Gwen sounded exactly like her dad and often regurgitated his words and phrases. 'Anyway, Daddy, you're always saying that some contact with germs is good for building my immune system so don't worry about it. I'll be just fine. It's not like I rubbed dog poo in my eyes, is it?'

'You can tell her daddy's a vet,' Carrie said.

Sean shot a look at Carrie and she held up her hands. He had often spoken about how it was good for Gwen to have contact with animals as it built her immune system, but he'd also warned her about things like the dangers of not washing her hands properly, especially after playing ball in the park because animal faeces carried worms that could cause blindness. It was a warning Carrie had heard as a child and repeated to Amy, and now Gwen was using it to illustrate her point. Carrie had to admit that she was filled with admiration for the clever little girl.

'No, it's not like you did that, Gwen,' Sean conceded. 'Another coffee, Carrie?'

'Go on then.'

Sean went to the counter and Carrie watched Gwen as she drained her drink then wiped her hand across her mouth, smearing the lipstick she'd already forgotten she was wearing.

Carrie sat back and relaxed, allowing the day's cleaning to drift away as she soaked up the café atmosphere. It was a chilly day but inside the café, it was cosy, the aromas of coffee, cake and toasted sandwiches filling the air along with the gentle hum of conversation. Parents and grandparents had collected children from school and brought them here for a Friday treat. In one corner, The Buggy Brigade sat at their usual table, empty prams lined up against the one wall, babies and toddlers on their laps or in highchairs. She and Tilly had often joked about The Buggy Brigade — it had been Tilly who'd named them that — but Carrie knew that Tilly had longed to become one of them. For quite some time, in fact. Now she never spoke about them, preferring to try to forget that she wanted to join their ranks, to walk with them along the coastal path, to run with them as she pushed one of those fancy running pushchairs and to join them for brunches and post-school run coffees. Tilly hadn't been able to conceive despite several rounds of IVF, and so she hadn't become one of The Buggy Brigade and Carrie's heart ached for her. Instead, Tilly had thrown herself into her career and filled her days with work, her nights with Netflix, gruelling workouts on that expensive exercise bike she'd bought and on long distance runs.

The door opened and Carrie's gaze travelled over to see who'd come in.

Instantly, heat rushed into her cheeks and she looked away, trying to calm herself.

'Aunty Carrie, why've you gone all red?' Gwen said loudly.

'Oh . . . I . . . I'm very warm.' Carrie placed her palms on her cheeks, wishing that the blush would fade.

'It's not that warm in here.' Gwen shook her head.

'It's a hormone thing that happens because of my age,' Carrie muttered, knowing full well that it had nothing to do with perimenopause or its older, more dramatic sister, menopause. Deep down, she didn't really feel old enough to face either one but knew that time was against her in that respect.

'What does that mean?' Gwen dropped her spoon in the glass mug and it clinked loudly.

Carrie looked up and her eyes met Ryan's. Her blush deepened.

'You've gone redder.' Gwen reached across the table and placed a hand on Carrie's forehead. 'I hope you're not coming down with something.'

'Me too.' Carrie couldn't drag her gaze away from Ryan as he approached the table.

'Hi,' he said, smiling. 'You OK?'

'Yes,' Carrie said, trying to think of a reason to explain her flushed state.

'And who's this young lady?' he asked as he looked at Gwen.

'I'm Gwen. Pleased to meet you.' Gwen held out a hand and Ryan shook it. 'And who are you?'

'I'm Ryan. I'm an old friend of Carrie's.'

'Aunty Carrie,' Gwen said as if to correct Ryan.

'This is your niece?' he asked.

'Yes. Gwen is Sean's daughter.'

'Well it's lovely to meet you, Gwen.'

Carrie watched as Gwen's eyes travelled over Ryan. 'Did you used to be Aunty Carrie's boyfriend?' she asked finally.

Now it was Ryan's turn to blush. 'Oh . . . uh . . . No. Sadly.' He glanced at Carrie and raised his eyebrows. 'Your aunty had a different boyfriend.'

'Oh.' Gwen sighed. 'I wondered if she was blushing because you two had a thing going. She has a photo of you in a box she keeps on top of her wardrobe.'

Ryan's eyes widened and Carrie covered her eyes for a moment, wishing the floor would open up and swallow her whole.

'Gwen . . . Ryan was just a friend.'

'That's nice. I have a friend called Jamie and sometimes he tries to kiss me in the yard but I don't let him. I don't have time for a boyfriend. I'm going to be a career woman like Aunty Carrie and Aunty Tilly.'

'Is that right?' Ryan nodded.

'They're both single,' Gwen said. 'Daddy said that's why they eat lots of chocolate.'

Ryan was grinning broadly now and Carrie was relieved to see Sean returning to the table. He set a tray of drinks down then turned to Ryan.

'Hi mate,' Ryan said. 'How're you doing?'

'Ryan . . . Davies?' Sean said.

'That's right. It's been a while.'

'It has indeed. It must be years.' Sean met Carrie's eyes then turned back to Ryan.

'I'm back for a few weeks to help my parents move and to clear out the house.'

'Nice one.' Sean nodded. 'I see you've met my daughter, Gwen?'

'Yes indeed. She's told me all about how she's going to be just like her aunties.'

Sean laughed. 'She certainly keeps me on my toes in the same way they do.'

'I can imagine,' Ryan said, winking at Carrie in a way that made her feel eighteen again. She knew it was his way of letting her know he was teasing but still, it made her stomach flutter. 'Anyway, I popped in for takeaway. My parents are packing the last of their things so I need to grab them something to eat then get back. I'll hopefully see you all again soon.'

Carrie bobbed her head, aiming to appear nonchalant although she was certain that was like closing the stable door after the horse had bolted, then Ryan headed to the counter.

'Haven't seen Ryan in years,' Sean said as he sat down.

'He made Aunty Carrie go as red as tomato sauce,' Gwen said.

'Did he now?' Sean smiled at Carrie. 'Is that because he looks like your favourite actor?'

Carrie feigned ignorance.

'What's his name? The guy that was Poldark? Aidan Turner, is it?' Sean laughed softly. 'He's got the hair, the dark eyes and everything else by the looks of him.'

'Cut it out,' Carrie said, glaring at her brother.

'Sorry!' Sean smiled. 'Just teasing you. It's nice to see you react to someone. Especially someone I know you used to be fond of.'

'I was not fond of him.' Carrie wrapped her hands around her mug. 'We were simply good friends.'

'I'll believe you but thousands

wouldn't.' Sean turned back to Gwen. 'Angel, do you think you could maybe go and wash a bit of that lipstick off? Just because it's all up your face now and I think the best way to wear makeup is the way Aunty Carrie does.'

'And how's that?' Carrie asked.

'Haven't I heard you say 'Less is more'? Or something like that? I'm sure you said that to Amy once when she was a teenager and she had a lot of black eye-shadow on.'

'Oh yes. When she was going through her goth phase.'

'That's right. So . . .' Sean nodded at Gwen. 'What do you think?'

'Tell you what, Gwen. Why don't you come with me and we can try to tidy your lipstick up a bit?'

'Only if you promise not to wash it *all* off.' Gwen cocked an eyebrow at Carrie.

'I promise. I just need to clean some of it off your chin.' Carrie winked at Sean.

'All right then. But later on, I get to give you a makeover.' Gwen held up a hand. 'Shake on it.'

'You drive a hard bargain, missy.' Carrie shook Gwen's hand then led her to the toilets, dreading the thought of one of Gwen's makeovers but prepared to agree if it meant they could clean some of the lipstick off her now. As they went to the sink though, and Carrie grabbed a paper towel, she caught sight of her reflection in the mirror and had to admit that she was just as red as her niece and she didn't have the excuse of lipstick.

Why on earth had Ryan affected her like that and how was she going to cope if every time she saw him, she went bright red? She was forty-five not fifteen and she needed to get a grip.

'He'd probably be your boyfriend if you asked him,' Gwen said as Carrie wiped at the lipstick on her chin.

'What?'

'Don't say what, it's rude,' Gwen admonished. 'And I was talking about that man . . . Ryan . . . with the dark hair. He'd say yes to a date.'

'Oh . . . I don't think so.'

'Bet you a tenner.'

'Uhhh . . . No thanks.'

'He likes you. I'm only six and I could see that he does.'

'Well . . . perhaps, but I'm happy as I am.'

'Sometimes change is a good thing,' Gwen said, scrunching up her face as Carrie scrubbed at her earlobe.

'Perhaps.' Carrie laughed. Gwen was six going on sixty sometimes and she suspected it was probably because the little girl spent so much time around adults. Even though she'd lost her mum when she was so young, she'd had her two loving aunties to help raise her and her devoted dad.

When Carrie had finished *tidying* Gwen's face, she washed her hands, and thought about what Gwen had said. Change could be a good thing but Carrie knew next to nothing about Ryan's life now and it would be presumptuous to think that he could be interested in her. After all, they'd never so much as kissed. They'd only ever been good friends.

Hadn't they?

# 6

'Here you go, boy!' Ryan threw the ball again and Eric chased after it. The beach was empty but then it was the last weekend of November. The sky was gunmetal grey, the sea choppy with white peaked waves, the air bitterly cold as it nipped at his nose and made his eyes water.

Ryan breathed in, enjoying the sensation as the cold air filled his lungs, cleansing and invigorating as a cold shower. One thing he'd definitely missed about Cwtch Cove was the beach, being able to walk while gazing at the sea and seemingly endless horizon, the cliffs that hugged the cove like protective arms. Either side of the beach, the land rose up to a plateau. On one side was Shore House Cottage and other rental properties and on the other was the clifftop development, something that hadn't been there when Ryan was growing up. The properties were modern, high-spec houses with large windows that overlooked the beach and the sea, and Ryan knew they didn't come cheap. But with views like that, he wasn't surprised.

Eric raced back to him and dropped the ball at his feet so he picked it up and threw it again. Ryan knew that his dog would play this game all day long if he could. In Bristol they played it in the park near his rented apartment but here they could enjoy time at the beach. In his navy padded gilet, Eric looked cuter than ever and Ryan felt that surge of love for the dog that always took him by surprise. He hadn't had a dog growing up but since he'd adopted Eric, he'd wondered why he hadn't got one before. The unconditional love that Eric gave him made up for the times when he had to get up in the middle of the night because Eric needed a wee, as well as for the fact that he couldn't go out at a moment's notice without thinking about Eric first. Having a dog was a big responsibility but Ryan enjoyed it; he'd tired of putting himself first a long time ago.

At the far end of the beach he spotted a man descending the ramp to the sand. He had a big dog with him that Ryan thought was a Labrador, but he couldn't be certain from this distance.

He kept walking, his boots crunching on the sand and flicking up droplets of water that sat on his jeans like glass beads before slowly sinking in and leaving dark stains.

As the man and dog got closer, he clipped Eric's lead to his harness to stop him racing towards what he could now see was definitely a yellow Labrador. The man raised a hand in greeting and Ryan realised it was Sean.

'Morning,' Sean said, pushing his beanie back on his head.

'Morning.'

'Nice day for a walk.' Sean gestured at the empty beach. 'Nothing like a chilly morning stroll to blow the cobwebs off, right?'

'Absolutely.' Ryan smiled. 'That your dog?'

Sean shook his head. 'She was brought

into the surgery yesterday. Her owner passed away and the owner's daughter would have taken her in but her husband has allergies.'

'What's her name?' Ryan asked as Eric strained at his lead to get close to the Labrador.

'Honey. It's OK, she's good with other dogs.'

'You going to keep her?' Ryan asked, letting Eric get close to Honey now so he could have a sniff.

'If we can't find a home for her, I might. The problem is that if I kept every animal that comes to the surgery in need of a home then I'd be overrun. Gwen gets attached to them too and that's why Honey is staying with one of our nurses until I can find her a home.'

Ryan stroked the dog's soft head, and she wagged her tail and peered up at him with big brown eyes.

'She'll find a home, won't she? She's beautiful.'

'I hope so.' Ryan nodded. 'Your boy seems to like her.'

'This is Eric. He's a rescue dog.' Ryan watched as Eric and Honey sniffed at each other, clearly fascinated. 'I was thinking about getting a companion for him.'

Sean's eyebrows rose slowly. 'I see. Well . . . Honey has been handed over to our care now so if you were interested in adopting her, we could have a chat about it.'

'I'd like that,' Ryan said, wondering if he was doing the right thing because it seemed rather impulsive. And yet, didn't things sometimes happen at the right time? Wasn't it sometimes good to take a chance? He'd taken a chance when he adopted Eric and that had worked out well. Perhaps adopting Honey would be a good thing too. After all, she was four, seemed calm, and Eric's initial meeting with her had gone well.

'Are you in Cwtch Cove for long?' Sean asked.

'I came to help my parents move and settle into their new home and I've rented a cottage until the new year. I'll probably stay until after Christmas so I can spend it with the folks and make the most of the beach.'

'So you could spend some time with Honey too and see how she gets on with Eric.'

'That would work.' Ryan inclined his head.

'Let me give you my number and we can sort something out this week if you like.'

'Great.' They exchanged numbers then Ryan slid his phone back into his pocket. 'It was good to see you yesterday at the café. Gwen is quite a character.'

'Isn't she just?' Sean laughed. 'She keeps me on my toes.'

'Carrie too by the look of it.'

'Yeah. My poor sister. That's the trouble with children . . . you can't say or do anything around them because they'll bring it back up at some point. You have any?'

'Nope. I guess I never found the right woman to settle down with.'

'I did but then . . .' Sean gazed out to

sea and for a moment he looked as if he'd gone far away in his mind. He sighed then met Ryan's gaze again. 'I lost her. Cancer.'

'I'm sorry for your loss. I can't imagine how difficult that must be.'

'Blood awful, mate, believe me. But . . . you know . . . What can you do? I have Gwen and my sisters, who are all amazing, and a job I love, so I just have to get on with it. That's all we can do, right?'

'Right.'

'You fancy catching up while you're here, drop me a text. Be good to chat properly.'

'Thanks. I'd like that.' Ryan smiled. 'We could bring the dogs on a play date.'

'Sounds like a plan. Perhaps I'll drag Carrie along too. She needs to get out more.'

Ryan's stomach flipped. A catchup with Carrie too? That would be perfect.

'Brilliant,' he said. 'Just name a day.'

'I'll try to remember to check with Carrie and message you.'

'Speak soon.'

As Sean walked away, Ryan unclipped Eric's lead then threw the ball ahead for him. As Eric chased after it, Ryan glanced behind him. He hadn't known Sean well when he'd lived in Cwtch Cove because the vet had been seven years younger than them and he'd seen him as Carrie's little brother, but he seemed like someone Ryan could be friends with. The fact that he was getting on with his life despite suffering such a huge loss was inspirational and Ryan admired him for running his business and being a father to a young child. Ryan didn't know if he'd have been able to do the same if he was in Sean's shoes.

Eric returned with the ball and dropped it then stared longingly after Sean and Honey.

'You like her, huh?' Ryan said.

Eric barked.

'Don't worry, boy, I'll get you another date with her. And then, perhaps, she could become your new sister. How does that sound?'

Eric pawed at his leg in response and Ryan laughed, not even minding that the dog had spread wet sand up his jeans.

# 7

On the drive to Shore House Cottage, Carrie's stomach was filled with butterflies. Part of her contract with Prime Properties included weekly cleaning of rental properties along with delivering clean bedding and towels. Prime Properties had a contract with a laundry company, so Carrie picked up bedding and towels from them then delivered them as she did her cleaning rounds.

She'd already done some of the properties on her list and today was heading up to Shore House while Levi and Daisy cleaned some of the private residences in the village. If it was a big job, like a house clearance or full rental property clean, they worked together, but some jobs didn't require the team so they spread out to get things done.

Carrie had considered asking Levi or Daisy to go to Shore House instead, but knew that if she did, they'd think it was strange and want to know why. Carrie always delivered the clean bedding and towels in her van, so a sudden change would arouse the suspicions of her team.

Besides which, she didn't mind the thought of seeing Ryan again. In fact, she wanted to see him again. If she could just get the blushing under control, she'd be fine.

Outside Shore House, she got the basket of bedding and towels out of the back of the van then went to the door. She knocked, knowing there was a chance that Ryan might be out anyway, in which case she'd use the key she'd been given. Alternatively, she had to hope that if he was home, there wouldn't be another towel-gate incident. Just the thought of it made Carrie smile.

Through the glass of the front door, she saw Ryan approaching. He paused to allow his dog to run ahead then opened it and smiled.

'Hello again, Carrie.'

'Hi.'

'You'll no doubt be relieved to see that

I'm dressed today.'

Carrie nodded. 'Very relieved.' *Don't blush!* 'I've got your bedding and some more towels here. I'll take any used ones away with me.'

'Thanks. I've set them aside ready.'

'Great.'

'Come on in.'

Ryan stepped back and Carrie entered the cottage, feeling the cosy warmth envelop her as she left the freezing morning air behind.

'Eric, give Carrie a break.'

Carrie looked down to see that the dog was staring up at her, one paw raised.

'Hello again, Eric.'

Eric barked then pawed at her leg, so she set the basket down and held out her hand. He sniffed at her palm then gave it a lick.

'That's a kiss, by the way,' Ryan said.

'I'm privileged.' Carrie stroked Eric's head. 'Thank you, Eric.'

'Let me get that.' Ryan picked up the basket. 'You want it upstairs?'

'That'd be great.'

'Although . . .' Ryan shook his head. 'I'm perfectly capable of swapping a few towels and changing the bed. I'd feel like a lazy sod if I expect you to do it every week.'

'It's my job. It's part of what Dust Busters does.'

'Yeah but . . . I don't want you to have to change my bed.' He chewed at his bottom lip. 'Let me grab the used towels and bedding and how about instead of you doing that, we have a coffee?'

'A coffee?'

'Yeah.' He shrugged. 'Be nice to catch up properly. Sean did mention getting together when I bumped into him at the beach but you're here now so . . .'

'Aren't you busy?' Carrie asked, feeling torn between hope — at the thought of having a coffee and a chat with him — and panic — at the thought of spending time with him. Would she be able to talk to him without blushing? Would they have anything to say?

'I've been up since six, so I've done some work already and I always have a mid-morning coffee break. Otherwise, I'd be a terrible employer, wouldn't I? I could sue myself for poor working conditions.'

Carrie smiled. 'OK then. That'd be lovely.'

'Go on through to the lounge and I'll be back in a bit.'

Carrie watched him pad up the stairs then she went through to the lounge. She gazed out of the window at the wonderful view of the cove. Even in winter, it looked beautiful, and she felt the softening in her gaze and the loosening in her shoulders that she always experienced when she looked at the sea. It was calming and soothing and she knew that she'd always want to live there, no matter what.

She glanced up at the creak of floorboards above her head, wondering what it would be like in the bedroom with Ryan staying there. The cottage already smelt different — a mix of his shower gel, aftershave and the washing detergent he used on his clothes. There was also the faint hint of garlic in the air from whatever he'd cooked recently and woodsmoke from the fire.

Feeling like she was being watched, she turned and saw that she was. Eric was sitting on the sofa staring at her. He had a toy rabbit under his front paws that looked old and worn.

'Is that your buddy, Eric?'

She approached the sofa and sat down next to the dog.

'He's lovely. Looks like you've had him a long time.'

Eric barked then picked the rabbit up and shook it from side to side.

Carrie reached out and took hold of the rabbit's foot and Eric tugged at it. She laughed as they played a game of tug of war while Eric growled playfully.

'Give him to me!' she said, tugging hard. There was a loud ripping sound and Eric staggered backwards while Carrie looked in horror at the rabbit's leg in her hand. 'Oh no.'

Eric blinked at her; the rabbit's body still gripped between his jaws. Carrie looked around, wondering if she should just hide the leg somewhere and feign ignorance or if she should blame Eric and say he'd got a bit rough with his toy.

'You know what, Eric,' she said, deciding that neither of the options was a good one. 'I have a sewing kit in the van for emergencies like this. I'll go and get it and we can get this leg back on in no time.'

She got up and went out to the van, hoping that Ryan wouldn't discover the dismembered rabbit before she went back inside. It was just typical that something like this — the destruction of a dog's beloved toy — would happen today when she had the chance to catch up with an old friend. Just typical . . .

* * *

Ryan plodded down the stairs with the basket of used towels and bedding and paused in the hallway. The front door was open and cold air rushed in. He went to the doorway and looked outside.

Carrie was leaning into the van. She wasn't leaving already, was she? Had he been upstairs for too long and she'd got fed up and decided to go?

Disappointment flooded through him. He'd been looking forward to speaking to her, to finding out more about what she'd been up to over the years. Perhaps he shouldn't be so keen to speak to her after how low he'd felt all those years ago, but then, they were both older now and a lot of time had passed. And it hadn't been Carrie's fault that she'd fallen for Grant. It had simply been life; one of those things.

He watched for a moment, wondering if she would leave without saying goodbye but then she closed the van and headed back to the cottage. She had something in her hand.

'Hi.' She came inside. 'I needed to get this from the car.' She held up a small rectangular tin.

'What is it?'

'My sewing kit.'

'Fancied doing some embroidery while

you were here, did you?' He laughed.

Carrie worried her bottom lip. 'Not exactly. See . . . I was playing with Eric and his rabbit and we both tugged a bit hard and—'

'Rabbit's leg came off?'

'Yes. How did you know?'

'It's not the first time.'

Carrie's eyes widened and she placed a hand on her chest. 'Thank goodness for that. I felt terrible. We had a little game of tug of war and next thing I knew; Rabbit was . . . partially legless.'

They both laughed hard and Carrie leant over, clutching her stomach. 'This . . . is . . . too funny. I was . . . so worried . . .'

'Don't be worried. These things happen. The amount of times Eric has licked, chewed, humped and shaken that rabbit until a piece of it has fallen off are too many to count. There's probably nothing other than a few pieces of cotton holding it together. Somewhere around here is a teddy bear that only has one leg although he might have left that one upstairs when we came down this morning.'

Carrie straightened up and wiped at her eyes with the back of a hand. 'I felt so bad for Eric. He looked horrified.'

'Probably worried it's his fault.' Ryan put the basket of washing down. 'Shall we go and check on him.'

'Please. And I'll see if I can perform emergency surgery on Rabbit.'

'Thank you.'

In the lounge, they found Eric sitting in front of the sofa with Rabbit. He looked up at them, blinked his big brown eyes and pawed at the rabbit.

'Oh Eric, I'm sorry.' Carrie knelt down and picked Rabbit up. 'Let me have a look at him and see if we can sew his leg back on.'

She located the leg and sat on the sofa with the soft toy on her lap.

'How about if I go and make some coffees and you and Eric can put Rabbit back together again?' Ryan said.

'I'd love a coffee, thank you.' Carrie smiled.

Ryan paused for a moment, gazing at his dog and his old friend, admiring how cute they looked sitting on the sofa together. It was something he'd imagined from time to time, having Carrie back in his life, but not like this — well, maybe a bit like this — and it was something he'd thought would never happen. After all, they'd only ever been friends, hadn't they?

And now, here she was, as if all those years had never happened.

* * *

'How's that, Eric?' Carrie asked as she tugged at the rabbit's leg to check it was firmly attached.

Eric moved closer to her on the sofa and sniffed at the toy then gently took it from her.

'You're a lovely boy, aren't you?' She reached out and stroked his ears and he leant towards her hand, clearly enjoying the fuss.

'I see you two are getting along well.'

Ryan set a tray with two mugs of coffee and a plate of mince pies on the table.

'I think so.' Carrie nodded. 'Mince pies, eh? I haven't had one this year yet.'

'Well then this can be your first.' Ryan gestured at the tray. 'Help yourself. Oh . . . I put milk in your coffee. Is that all right? I was on autopilot.'

'Milk is good but I don't take sugar.'

'Sweet enough,' he said, then his cheeks turned pink.

'Something like that.' She reached for her coffee and cradled it between both hands.

Ryan picked up his mug then sat on the other sofa. 'So how have you been, Carrie? Over the years, I mean.'

'I'm good. I didn't go away to university, as you know, but I worked a variety of different jobs here. I was with Grant, of course . . .' She found herself gritting her teeth together instinctively. 'But, well . . . that didn't work out.'

'I'm sorry about that. Gwen said the other day that you were single but other than that . . . I didn't know anything about you splitting up.'

Carrie blew on her coffee then took a sip. 'We were together for twelve years in total. We had our daughter, Amy, when we were twenty-five. She's away at university now.'

'Wow! You have an adult daughter. That seems crazy, doesn't it? That we're old enough to have adult children.'

'It does. I can hardly believe it myself even though I have photographs of her everywhere at home. And on my phone.' Carrie pulled her phone from her pocket and showed Ryan her lock screen. 'This was us together last time she was home.'

Ryan looked at the photo then at Carrie. 'She's a lot like you.'

'So people say. I find that a huge compliment as I think she's the most beautiful person in the world.' She smiled. 'She's the best thing I've ever done.'

'What's she doing at uni?'

'Pharmacology. She's very bright. She's seeing someone now though and I'm hoping that he's a kind man. He's doing the same course and she must like him because she's not coming home for Christmas.' She took a sip of coffee. 'For the first time ever.'

'How do you feel about that?'

Carrie sighed. 'Sad. Disappointed. Happy that she's independent enough to be able to live her own life. A whole bunch of emotions that I can't really pin down. Parenthood is wonderful but it can be tough. Sorry . . .' She bit her lip. 'I could be telling you something you already know.'

'I don't have children. This might sound a bit sad but . . . I've never been in a particularly serious relationship.'

'What? Never?'

He shook his head then pushed a hand through his dark brown hair. The light caught the glint of silver in amongst the brown. 'I just never met the right woman after I left Cwtch Cove.' When his eyes met hers, she swallowed hard. What did he mean? *After* he left? 'Don't get me wrong. I had relationships but nothing that lasted or that I wanted to pursue for longer than a few months at a time. I've been happy and had a great life so far. I love my job, love Eric, and my parents are still around. Sometimes I wonder what it would have been like to have a family and a special someone but it just doesn't happen for some people.'

'I guess not.' Carrie sipped her coffee. 'I . . . I've been single since Grant and I split.'

'What happened?' Ryan grimaced. 'Sorry. That popped out. It's a personal matter so please don't answer.'

'No, it's OK. It's no secret and most people in the village know. Grant was always a bit of a lad, as you might remember. He spent a lot of time with his mates, going on trips with them abroad, as well as going out quite often with them. He was always car mad and used to go to watch Formula 1 and other races, as well as doing up cars at the garage and selling them on. We never got married even though he asked me more than once. I don't know what it was, but it just didn't feel right. We were young when we had Amy and I was so caught up in being a mum that I wasn't that concerned about what he did. In that way, I guess I was at fault. But anyway, we drifted apart as many couples do. He had an affair and went on to marry the woman he was seeing. They live in Cardiff with their twins who are about . . . ten now. I think. Yes, that's what Amy told me earlier this year. They'd just turned ten. So . . .' She held up her free hand. 'What can you do?'

'Grant was always an idiot.'

'What?' Carrie's eyebrows shot up her forehead. 'But you two were good friends when we were at school.'

'Yeah but that was when we were kids. And the three of us were friends, not just me and him. It didn't matter then that he was a bit of . . . as you called him . . . a lad. He was young and he wasn't hurting anyone but to cheat when you had a daughter together.' He shook his head. 'That's idiotic.'

'It happens, Ryan.' She'd had years to come to terms with Grant's affair and sometimes she could feel calm about it, as if it wasn't an issue anymore, but at others, the old hurt could still rear its head. 'We drifted apart and I can't deny that I was upset at the time. That I raged at him at the time. But when I calmed down and had time to think about it all, I was actually relieved to let him go. We didn't make each other happy. I've actually been far happier without him.'

'So you said you've been single . . . for fifteen years?'

'Is that embarrassing?' She shrugged. 'I don't know. I've been so busy raising my daughter, running my business and being there for my siblings that I've not had time to think about it that much.' She finished her coffee, wondering why she was telling him all this and how it was so easy to speak to him. 'Well, I've tried not to because there's no point dwelling on what you haven't got, is there? I had a few dates over the years but . . . It just seemed like too much hard work.'

Ryan laughed. 'Dating is hard work. All that getting dressed up, wondering if you'll have anything to talk about . . . worrying about how the night will end. Will they call you again? Won't they? Did you bore them? Did you have food stuck in your teeth when you smiled at them across the table in the restaurant?'

'Exactly.' She gazed at him, curious about how he could ever worry about those things. Behind his glasses, his eyes were a rich brown, his smile warm and friendly. He was gorgeous and she knew he was a nice person — or he used to be — and he was easy to be with. She had always felt so comfortable with him. 'I'd rather be in my pjs with a mug of hot chocolate and a good series on Netflix these days.'

'Sounds perfect to me.' He put his mug on the tray. 'Look at that. We drank our coffee and didn't eat the mince pies. And they're M&S ones too.'

'Perhaps we should have another coffee then? Be such a shame to waste good mince pies.'

*And I don't want to leave yet.*

'I'll put the kettle on.' He took the mug from her hand and their fingers brushed.

Carrie gasped as a spark of something rushed through her. His pupils dilated and Carrie had to force herself to stay seated as if an unfamiliar force was trying to drag her towards him.

When Ryan had returned to the kitchen, she sat back on the sofa and turned to Eric who was cuddling his rabbit next to her.

'What just happened, boy? What was that?'

Eric blinked at her then yawned, making her smile.

But as she folded her hands in her lap, she couldn't help wondering why her heart was still beating so hard and whether Ryan had felt it too.

# 8

Carrie pulled her black woolly hat on in front of the mirror in the hallway. She couldn't believe it was the first of December already. The years seemed to fly past now, and Christmas arrived quickly, often taking her by surprise.

She opened the small pot of lip gloss she'd added to her shopping trolley that week and applied some to her lips. It had a rose tint to it but also moisturised her lips and stopped them getting chapped in the cold.

*And it looks good . . .*

She turned around, wondering where that voice had come from. But when she looked into her own eyes in the mirror, she could see that something was different about her. In the three days since she'd had coffee with Ryan, she'd had a new spring in her step. Not that she moped around feeling sorry for herself normally, but something about spending time with Ryan had made her feel . . . different. Almost younger, as if a part of herself that she'd believed to be long gone had been given a boost. Reignited like a flame, even.

When they were teenagers, Ryan had seemed so serious and quiet, not like the energetic alpha male Grant appeared to be. Ryan had glasses back then too and thick dark hair that flopped over his forehead. He carried himself awkwardly, as if his body parts didn't quite work in sync. Grant, in contrast, had walked with a swagger, been driving as soon as he passed his test at seventeen and had the confidence of a celebrity. Carrie had liked Ryan and Grant; they'd both been her friends before anything else had developed and she'd cared about them equally. But Grant had shown interest in her, gone all out to impress her, while Ryan had been kind and caring but in quieter, less obvious ways. Carrie had never felt certain that Ryan saw her as anything other than a friend, whereas Grant made it clear that he fancied her.

It had been a long, hot summer the year they'd all turned eighteen, a summer of swimming, beach barbecues and cheap cider. Carrie felt blissfully alive, invincible in her youth and vitality. She'd read romance novels voraciously as she lay on a towel on the sand, sipping ice cold Coke from glass bottles. Her skin had turned golden, her hair grown lighter from the sun and freckles had spread across her nose and cheeks. She'd spent time with all her friends that summer, and revelled in it, aware that it was the summer before everything would change. When autumn had arrived, their friendship group *had* changed, as many of them went off to university or began apprenticeships or jobs. Ryan went off to university but Grant and Carrie remained in Cwtch Cove, and one night, they became more than just friends. By the Christmas of that year, Grant and Carrie were officially a couple, so when Ryan had come home to see his parents, everything had been different. Carrie couldn't even recall seeing Ryan much after that. Had he stayed away from Cwtch Cove then? She'd been caught up in her relationship, determined to give it all her effort because Grant had been attentive back then, had convinced her he loved her. And she still believed he had, even now, in his own way. But things changed, life changed, people changed. It was just how things were. The love between Carrie and Grant had left the building, so to speak, and that had been that.

She pulled her gloves from her pockets and put them on before opening the door. Outside, it was dark and cold, a perfect early December evening. Frost was already settling on cars and grass making everything seem to sparkle and her breath came out like puffs of smoke that disappeared into the air. This evening was the turning on of the village lights. The village committee at Cwtch Cove still waited until the first of December to turn the lights on and she was glad because it marked the transition from November into the festive month. Even at forty-five, she still got a jolt of excitement at the thought that Christmas was on the horizon. She loved Christmas and the time it promised with family and friends, although, of course, she would desperately miss Amy this year.

During the short walk to the village green, she thought about the time she'd spent with Ryan a few days ago. It had been so easy to talk to him, like all that time had never passed since they last spoke at length. She'd always been able to talk to him and had missed him after he left for university, but Grant had been around, and Carrie only had room for one man in her heart at a time.

But now, Ryan was back, and Carrie felt different. Everything was different. When their fingers had brushed as he'd taken her mug, that jolt she'd experienced had been . . . unfamiliar. Incredibly pleasant. She wanted to know if it had been a one off, a fluke, or if it would happen if they touched again. Ryan had said he'd come to the turning on of the lights this evening and Carrie was looking forward to seeing him. The fact that he would be there had nothing to do with the extra time she'd taken getting ready this evening, or why she'd bought a new pair of black leather boots for the occasion. Nothing at all.

She released a long sigh. Who exactly was she trying to fool?

* * *

'It's so lovely to have you here this year, Ryan dear,' his mum said, a huge smile on her face.

'It's nice to be here.' Ryan hugged her.

'And thanks for all the help with the move, son.' His dad patted his back. 'It made it all much easier.'

'No problem. There's just the things of mine left at the house now so I'll take those up to the cottage and then Dust Busters can do a thorough clean.' Ryan had spoken to Carrie about hiring her company to clean his parents' house to save them having to do it. They'd both been sad when they'd taken the last of their things from the house this week and he thought that returning to it to clean and seeing it empty would be difficult for them. He felt protective and wanted to look out for them, kind of how they'd looked out for him over the years. Was this what happened to everyone? As you aged, you took over the caring role and looked after your parents in the way they once looked after you?

He watched them now, dressed in thick wool coats, hats and gloves, and his heart squeezed. They definitely looked smaller than they used to, as if time was shrinking them. Part of it was because he'd grown, he knew, but part of it was ageing. Time slipped away like sand in an hourglass and as much as you might wish it was different, you couldn't stop it. All you could do was to make the most of each moment, treasure the time you had with loved ones and live for today.

He caught sight of Carrie approaching the green and his stomach flipped. He was catapulted back almost thirty years to the Christmas he was sixteen. He'd shyly asked her if she'd be attending the turning on of the lights and she'd said she was taking her younger siblings. Back then, Ryan had been too shy to ask her to be his date even if it did mean Sean and Tilly would be tagging along. He'd lacked the confidence to tell Carrie how he felt. It was innocent back then, though, a young emotion that he couldn't quite explain, even to himself. But when she'd arrived at the green with Sean and Tilly, Ryan had spotted her and decided to ask if they all wanted hot chocolates. And then, just as he'd almost reached them, Grant had appeared as if from out of nowhere with a tray of drinks and fresh donuts. Ryan had slunk away, stunned that his friend had got there first, confused about what Grant's motives were because until that point, Grant hadn't said a word about fancying Carrie. In fact, Ryan had actually told Grant a few days before that he was thinking about trying to pluck up the courage to ask Carrie to go to the cinema with him, although he didn't know if he had the nerve to do it. Grant had told him he should ask her, encouraged him with a friendly pat on the back, so what was he doing staying glued to her side at the turning on of the lights?

Now, Ryan knew. It was crystal clear that Grant had listened to Ryan and possibly it was then that he'd seen Carrie in a different light and decided to pursue her himself. It hadn't happened immediately, but Grant had tried to sow seeds in her mind and possibly in Ryan's, because the next day at school, Grant's swagger had an extra bounce to it. When Grant had seen Ryan, he'd stared at him hard, as if waiting for Ryan to confront him about what he'd done. But Ryan hadn't had the courage to try to articulate whatever it was that he was feeling for Carrie, and so, he'd stepped back. If he regretted anything in life, it was that. He'd cared for Carrie a long time ago but Grant had pushed him aside and Ryan had let him. The so-called jock had beaten the so-called geek, just like in the movies.

But now, Ryan thought, as he saw Carrie greeting her siblings and niece, perhaps it was time for the geek to come out on top. Perhaps now, Ryan and Carrie could have the chance they'd lost all that time ago. If Carrie liked him in that way, of course. Ryan wasn't going to take anything for granted. Carrie was special and she should be treated like a queen. Ryan knew for sure that he didn't want to regret not taking this chance and allow any more precious time to slip away. He hadn't found another woman he cared about and perhaps that been because he'd never got over Carrie.

* * *

Carrie sipped the sweet, spiced wine Sean had given her in a recyclable cardboard cup and felt it warm her right through. Next to her, Gwen was devouring a freshly cooked donut while Sean held her hot chocolate along with his own.

'I'm so excited!' Gwen said between bites. 'This means that it's not long until Santa comes with my lovely pressies.'

'You're right,' Carrie said. 'I can't wait for your school concert.'

'Daddy has bought me a beautiful dress and I look amazing in it,' Gwen said with the confidence of a six-year-old.

'I'm sure you do.' Carrie smiled at Sean. 'Well done, Daddy Bear.'

He laughed. 'I can put my hand to anything.'

'Does anyone want another drink?' Tilly asked. She looked very smart this evening in a purple wool coat, black ankle boots and black beret, Carrie thought. She'd come straight from work and Carrie was hoping to get her home later on so she could feed her. She'd made a root vegetable soup and garlic bread to warm them up afterwards.

'Go on then. That wine went down a treat,' Carrie handed her the cup.

'I'm fine thanks.' Sean shook his head. 'And Gwen hasn't touched hers yet. Too busy munching donuts.'

Tilly walked away and Carrie looked around. Her eyes landed on Ryan and she found he was gazing right at her. She waved and he waved in return, making her heart skip a beat.

'I'll be back in a moment. Just going to say hello to someone,' she said.

'No problem.' Sean nodded.

*What am I doing?*

Carrie's stomach was in knots as she approached Ryan and his parents, but she was determined to make her old friend feel welcome.

* * *

'Is that Carrie?' Ryan's mum pointed.

'It is indeed.' His stomach fluttered.

'Hello, dear.' His mum smiled. 'How are you?'

'I'm really good, thanks,' Carrie said. 'And you?'

'All good here, thank you.' Ryan's mother raised her mulled wine. 'Enjoying a little tipple.'

'The wine's delicious,' Carrie said.

'We'll all be tipsy,' Ryan's father said. 'Good job we're not turning the lights on.'

'I can't take them anywhere,' Ryan said to Carrie with an exaggerated wink, making his parents chuckle. 'You here with your family?'

Carrie nodded. 'Gwen is so excited about Christmas that I'm worried she might pop.'

'Ahhh . . . I remember Ryan being like that,' his mother said. 'He was so excited one year that he wet the bed. He was trying to stay awake to see Santa but he must've passed out in the early hours and he'd drunk too much squash and then, around dawn, I heard those awful words . . . 'Mum, I had a wet night.'' She pulled a face.

'What?' Ryan frowned in horror. 'When?'

'Oh . . . you were about four or five.'

'Mum! That's not relevant. I was clearly very young.'

'I'm teasing you, Ryan,' she replied.

'You were about fifteen.'
'Mum!' Ryan shook his head. 'Cut it out.'
She laughed mischievously. 'Talking of the loo . . . I think I'd better pay a visit before the lights are turned on. The cold isn't helping.'
'I'll walk with you,' his father said. 'It's frosty and we don't want you slipping.'
As his parents walked away, Carrie said, 'That's so sweet. Your dad is such a gentleman and clearly cares a lot about your mum.'
'Pair of old romantics they are.' Ryan smiled. 'I worry about them and feel I should be around to help them more.'
'I'm sure they wouldn't want you to give up your exciting life in Bristol.'
He laughed. 'Exciting life? Lonely life more like.' He caught himself and gritted his teeth. 'I didn't mean to say that. I don't really get lonely . . . well, not all the time. There's Eric, of course, and he's brilliant company, and I'm busy with work. But I don't have any close friends there or family, so it's kind of just me

and Eric.'

Carrie was gazing into his eyes as he spoke and he wondered what she thought about him. Did he sound sad and pathetic, or could she understand what he was saying? She had family and friends in the village and probably didn't know what loneliness felt like.

'I can see how that would get lonely and why you'd worry about your parents. My dad passed away ten years ago and I miss him dreadfully. My mother lives in Italy and . . . I don't know if you remember much about her, but she was never a motherly mum. She was very . . . self-involved. She wasn't horrid but she wasn't like the mums my friends had in school. Not like your mum. I couldn't be there for her even if I wanted to. I do have Sean and Tilly here though, and Gwen, of course. But even so . . . I still feel lonely sometimes.' She lowered her gaze and stared into space.

'Perhaps it's just the human condition.' Ryan shrugged. 'We're all destined to feel lonely.'

'I don't think it is.' Carrie met his gaze again. 'I think that we can have deep connections with family and friends and even after everything that happened with Grant . . . I believe we can have a deep romantic connection. With the right person, that is.' She held his gaze and his breath caught in his throat. Was there a message in this for him? He took a step towards her and found himself reaching for her hand. He took it and a spark shot through him, making him exhale sharply. Carrie's eyes widened and her lips parted.

'Aunty Carrie!' Gwen crashed into Carrie, making her wobble and Ryan looked away quickly, trying to compose himself.

'Oh! Hey, Gwen.'

'What are you doing?' Gwen tugged on Carrie's hand. 'The lights will be on in a minute and you're standing over here staring at . . . Ryan. Come back to Daddy.'

'Of course.' Carrie shook her head as if to clear her thoughts and Ryan knew how she felt. 'Uh . . . Ryan . . . Do you want to come with us?'

He did. Desperately. He wanted to know what had almost happened in that moment when the world around them had seemed to blur and they'd been like the only two people at the green. The years had fallen away and they'd been like the teenagers they once were; free from baggage and social restraint; free to do whatever they wanted to do — if only they were brave enough. If only they really understood what it was that they felt for each other. And then the moment had evaporated and they were thrust back into reality.

'I'd love to join you but I . . .uh . . . should spend some time with Mum and Dad.'

'Well, when they come back, bring them over and you can all join us.'

'Yes! Brilliant idea. Thanks.' He blushed at his eager response but Carrie was smiling at him with a softness in her gaze.

'Don't be long,' she whispered before

she let Gwen lead her away.

'Don't worry,' he replied. 'I've been too long already and don't plan on wasting another minute.'

* * *

When the lights were turned on, all around Carrie people *oohed* and *ahhed* and she grinned with delight. Gwen jumped up and down, clapped her hands and squealed when the star at the top of the large tree at the centre of the green glowed brightly.

'Now it really feels like Christmas!' Gwen said.

'It does,' Carrie replied as she took it all in. The village committee had outdone themselves this year. Lights flashed around the tree, thousands of twinkling fairy lights were draped between lampposts and around stone planters, and mini trees covered in lights had been set in pots in front of shops and the village hall. 'It's beautiful.'

She looked at Ryan and found his

eyes fixed on her. He leant closer and whispered, '*You're* beautiful.'

Her first instinct was to protest as she always did, always had whenever someone complimented her. But the honesty in his gaze made her stop and decide to accept it. So she smiled and inclined her head in thanks, enjoying the way she felt when Ryan was around.

# 9

'How about that one?' Gwen asked as she pointed at an enormous tree.

'I don't think we'll get that one in the van.' Carrie laughed.

Carrie had brought Gwen Christmas tree shopping at a local farm. Sean was at the surgery conducting an emergency Saturday morning operation, so Carrie was taking care of Gwen. It had been over a week since the lights had been turned on at the green and in that time she'd cleaned out Ryan's parents' home with her team, along with completing her usual cleaning rounds and getting some Christmas shopping done for her family. Now that Amy wouldn't be home for Christmas, she had considered trying to find something small enough to post to her. When she'd said this to Ryan at his parents' house, he'd suggested sending Amy and her boyfriend a festive hamper from an online company and Carrie had thought it was a brilliant idea. She'd found a company that made up gourmet baskets and ordered one. Apart from Amy, she needed to get something for Sean, Gwen and Tilly, as well as for her cats. Christmas wasn't Christmas if the cats didn't get a stocking each. She'd forgotten one year and her cats had both sulked. She wondered if Ryan got gifts for Eric.

'That one?' Gwen pointed at a smaller tree.

'That one looks good.' They went closer to take a proper look at it. 'What's its name?'

'Uhhh . . . It's a Nor–man fire.'

Carrie bit the inside of her cheek. 'Almost. Look at the letters with me.' She ran a finger over the words. 'It says it's a N-o-r-d-*mann* F-i-r. So put that together and it's Nordmann Fir.' Carrie leant in and sniffed. 'I can't smell anything though. Can you? Perhaps something very faint?'

Gwen sniffed the tree. 'Nope.'

'I like the scent of a real tree so I don't

think that one's right.'

'Better keep looking then.' Gwen tugged at Carrie's hand. 'Or we'll never find one in time and you'll be an old saddo on Christmas Eve.'

'I beg your pardon!' Carrie stopped walking and looked at her niece. Gwen was giggling so Carrie tickled her chin. 'You're such a tease, Gwen.'

They walked between the rows of trees and Carrie read the names.

'This is a Norway Spruce. Is it cat friendly, Gwen?' She pointed at the sign.

'Yes.'

'And how do you know that?'

'The sign shows a cat and a dog with a tick next to it.'

'That's right. Clever girl.' Carrie had been encouraging Gwen to read, turning a shopping trip into an educational experience. It had worked with Amy when she was younger, and it seemed to be working with Gwen too. 'And does it smell good?'

'Yes, it does! This one is purr-fect.'

Carrie laughed. 'I like what you did

there. Let's get one of these then.'

Once she'd got a trolley, she loaded the tree onto it ready to push it to the counter.

'I wish Daddy would get a real tree.'

'You have a tree already.'

'I know but it's a pretend one.'

'I think it's a lovely tree.'

Carrie knew why Sean kept hold of the tree he had. He'd bought it with Lara the Christmas before she got ill. The sentimental value it had surpassed any desire he might have to get a real tree for a change and Carrie wasn't sure he'd ever be able to get rid of it. Not wanting to share this with Gwen and upset her, Carrie said, 'I think that with him being a vet, he needs to make sure he keeps the house as a safe environment if he has to bring any animals home over Christmas.'

'Well then he could get a Norway Spruce like you.' Gwen crossed her arms over her chest and pouted.

'You can come and see mine whenever you want.' Carrie stroked Gwen's cheek

'Aunty Carrie . . .' Gwen looked up at

her. 'I think I miss my mummy.'

'Oh sweetheart . . .' Carrie crouched down and took Gwen's hands. 'I'm sure you do.'

'I have this . . . pain here.' Gwen rubbed at her chest. 'It makes my eyes sting too.'

'Your mum was very lovely and you're bound to miss her.'

'But also . . .' Gwen frowned. 'I don't remember her very well. I look at the photo album in my room that Daddy made for me, and I can see my mummy holding me in photos but . . . I can't always remember her face if I don't look at the album. Sometimes . . . I remember the sound of her voice and how she smelt.'

'We all forget what people look like. I sometimes can't remember exactly what my dad's face was like, so I look at photos too.'

'Do you?'

Carrie nodded.

'But you were old when your daddy died.'

'Well . . . I was thirty-five. So yes, I did have more time with him than you had with your mummy . . . But even so, I need to look at photos sometimes to remember his face properly.'

'I wish my mummy hadn't died when I was only two. I wish I'd been thirty-five so I could know her better.'

'I know.' Carrie wrapped her arms around Gwen and hugged her tight. Gwen's eyelashes tickled Carrie's cheek. She was such a precious little girl and Carrie wished she could wave a magic wand and make everything all right for her and for Sean again. The fact that she couldn't do this hurt, and she worried constantly about Sean and Gwen.

When Gwen pulled away, her eyes were glistening, and the tip of her nose was pink.

'Don't tell my daddy.'

'Tell him what?'

'That I was sad. I don't want to make him sad.'

'It's OK to let people know when you feel sad, Gwen. You don't have to hide it or try to protect people. Your daddy is a grownup and you're a little girl.'

'I know but . . .' Gwen pulled a tissue from her pocket and dabbed at her eyes. 'I don't want him to be sad, now. Not at Christmas.'

'I won't tell him.' Carrie kissed Gwen's forehead then pulled her hat down a bit lower to keep her warm. 'But you can tell him yourself if you feel sad. It's good to talk about how you're feeling.'

'OK.' Gwen blinked up at Carrie. 'Come on then let's get some decorations for this tree.'

'Good plan. And while we're doing that, let's find some for you to take home for your tree.'

The smile Gwen flashed at Carrie told her she'd said the right thing.

* * *

Ryan walked towards the rows of Christmas trees at the farm. He'd driven the twenty minutes from Cwtch Cove because although his parents had offered him their old tree for the cottage, he thought he'd like to get a real one. Eric was with his parents at their new flat waiting for a few pieces of the steak his dad was cooking for dinner. Eric really was like a spoilt grandchild.

He walked under a wooden archway decorated with holly, ivy and twinkling fairy lights and was about to head for the trees when he spotted Carrie and Gwen.

'Carrie!' He waved and she smiled in return so he jogged over to them.

'Fancy seeing you here.'

'I thought I'd get a tree for the cottage.'

Her eyebrows met. 'Ooh . . . Have you checked that you're allowed?'

'Why? Is it against the rental rules?' he asked.

'It might be. Just in case the pine needles drop and make a mess. I doubt the cleaning company will be too happy about that.' She shook her head but her shoulders were shaking.

'Are you teasing me?'

'Of course I am. Get yourself a nice

tree.' She met his eyes and he rocked on his feet. In her grey wool hat, black fleece, jeans and boots, she wasn't dressed up but he thought she looked beautiful. Her eyes were an intense blue as if mirroring the clear morning sky and the cold had brought colour to her cheeks.

'You're staring at Aunty Carrie all funny again,' Gwen said, snapping him from his thoughts.

'Am I?' He looked at Gwen. 'In what way?'

Gwen rolled her eyes. 'I don't know, I'm only six but you look funny when you stare at her. Like . . . she's a chocolate cake or something.'

'Oh.' He rubbed at the back of his neck. 'Is that right. Goodness . . . I'm sorry about that, Carrie. I don't think you are a chocolate cake.'

Carrie was laughing. 'I've been compared to worse things. I guess I am a bit like a chocolate cake . . . round, soft and, dare I say, sweet? It's probably because I eat too many cakes.' She shrugged.

'You look pretty tasty to me.' Ryan

gasped. 'Oh . . . I didn't mean that I meant . . . uh . . . you look great. Gorgeous. Uh . . . curves in all the right places. Oh god! I can't think straight.'

*Shut up, Ryan, before you dig an even deeper hole.*

'Thank you. I'll take all of those as compliments. I don't get many these days.' Carrie winked. 'You want help choosing a tree?'

'But we're meant to be getting decorations!' Gwen tapped Carrie's arm.

'We are but we could help Ryan then get decorations for our tree and for his.'

'OK then.' Gwen nodded. 'Would you like us to come and help you decorate your tree, Ryan?'

'If you have time later today, I would like that very much.'

'Good!' Gwen took hold of his hand. 'Because my daddy is operating on a rabbit with a bad foot and he said he might be there all day if another animal comes in, so we can spend the time with you and Eric. Where is Eric?' she asked looking around. 'Has he run away?'

'No, thank goodness. He's with my parents. But I'll pick him up after I've got a tree so you can see him later.'

'That's all right then. I was worried.' Gwen pointed at the trees. 'Let me tell you which trees are best.'

'Great, thanks.'

Ryan grinned at Carrie as Gwen led him away. He hadn't expected to have company this morning but he was delighted, especially now he knew he'd have company to decorate the tree too. And very nice company it was indeed.

* * *

'Aunty Carrie?' Gwen rubbed her eyes.

'Yes?'

'Could I have another—' Gwen yawned. 'Another biscuit, please?'

'I think you might need to go home soon, poppet.'

'Noooooo.' Gwen shook her head. 'I'm fine.' She yawned again.

'You're tired. But you can have another biscuit and while you get one, I'll let your dad know I'll take you home.'

'Thank you!' Carrie ran off to the kitchen leaving Ryan and Carrie sitting on the sofa.

'The tree looks amazing. Thanks so much.' Ryan smiled.

'You're very welcome.'

After Carrie and Gwen had helped Ryan choose a tree, they'd helped him pick out some decorations. While Ryan took his tree back to Shore House, they made their way back to Carrie's. Carrie and Gwen had decorated Carrie's tree, had some lunch, then come up to help Ryan and they'd been there all afternoon. It was early evening now and Ryan had lit a fire in the grate and turned on the tree lights. The lounge was warm and cosy and it wasn't just Gwen who was tired; Carrie felt like she could easily drop off too.

'I'll just let Sean know.' She held up her phone and rang her brother. When she ended the call, she said, 'Sean insisted on coming to pick her up. He said I should stay here and relax.'

'Brilliant!' Ryan's eyes lit up. 'I can make us some supper if you like.'

'Supper?' Carrie laughed. 'I'm still full of the pizza you made.' Ryan had whipped up some homemade pizzas for dinner along with sweet potato fries and they'd been delicious. He seemed to have quite a talent in the kitchen.

'How about some cheese and crackers instead? I have some olives and a creamy brie.'

'Sounds great.'

'Plus I have a bottle of red there that will go perfectly with them. And . . . we could watch a Christmas movie.'

Carrie nodded vigorously. 'That sounds like a perfect evening to me.'

'Me too.' He held her gaze, his eyes filled with something she couldn't quite pin down. It was hopeful and intense. It made her stomach flutter and her heart race. It made her feel young and yet mature all at the same time, as if this man saw the girl she'd once been and the woman she was now. Most of all, in his eyes what she saw made her feel that he cared for her exactly as she was.

'Aunty Carrie!' Gwen skipped back into the room. 'Eric pinched my biscuit and took it to his bed!'

'Oh no!' Carrie stood up. 'It wasn't a chocolate chip one, was it?'

'No.' Gwen shook her head. 'It was a shortbread.'

'Well that was naughty of Eric.' Ryan stood up. 'I'll go and have a word with him.'

They all went to the kitchen and found Eric munching away on the biscuit, drool flying everywhere.

'Eric!' Ryan wagged a finger. 'Did you take that from Gwen?'

Eric's little tail wiggled.

'Here you are, Gwen, have another one.' Ryan held out the plate.

'Thank you, Ryan.' Gwen picked a shortbread biscuit.

'You're welcome. I don't know why he did that though.' Ryan knitted his brows. 'He doesn't normally take things unless someone offers them to him. Mind you, he is quite spoilt, so he doesn't really need to steal.'

'Gwen?' Carrie said. 'Did you offer Eric the biscuit?'

'A little bit.' Gwen chewed her lip.

'A little bit?'

'I held it out and said he could take a little bit but he took the whole bloody thing.'

'Gwen, don't say bloody. Your daddy's told you about that.'

'Sorry!' Gwen peered at Carrie and swayed slightly from side to side. 'It slipped out accidentally.'

A knocking at the front door made Eric bark, jump from his bed and race to the door.

'I'm not even sure why his bed is in here,' Ryan said, scratching his chin. 'It was in the lounge and upstairs he often lies next to me on the bed.'

'Perhaps he moved it in there?' Carrie shrugged.

'Yeah, perhaps. Better get the door.'

After Ryan had gone, Carrie said, 'Gwen, did you move Eric's bed in here?'

'Yes. He was sitting in it and I was

dragging him around as we played sailors.'

'Sailors?'

'Yes. He was in a boat and the floor was the sea.'

'Ahhhh.' Carrie nodded. 'That explains it then.'

Gwen went to the doorway and peered into the hallway. 'It's Daddy!'

Carrie followed Gwen out to the front door.

'Come on in, Sean,' Ryan said. 'Fancy a coffee?'

'Thanks for the offer but I have to get back.' Sean yawned. 'Gwen had us both up early this morning then I had two emergency surgeries. A rabbit came in with an injured foot and a dog that had swallowed a ball. Both successful, thankfully, but I'm shattered now.'

'Here's your coat, Gwen.' Carrie helped her niece into her coat then put her hat over her hair.

'Thank you.' Gwen hugged Carrie tight.

'Thanks for having Gwen today.' Sean

smiled. 'Hopefully she'll sleep tonight. All night.'

'Daddy, you should see Aunty Carrie's tree. It's the most beautiful thing ever and Ryan's is nice too.'

'It is,' Ryan said. 'I was very lucky to have excellent help.'

Sean smiled. 'Come on then, Gwen. See you tomorrow, Carrie. Bye Ryan.'

Ryan closed the door. 'Fancy opening that wine now?'

'Definitely.' Carrie smiled.

Twenty minutes later, they had a tray of crackers and cheese on the coffee table in front of the sofa and a large glass of red wine each. They were sitting on the sofa together and Carrie had her legs curled up underneath her. After some deliberation, they'd decided to watch *Home Alone*. Ryan had seemed open to watching a romantic comedy, but Carrie had remembered that he'd loved Home Alone when they were younger, so encouraged him to watch that.

She sat back on the sofa and raised her glass. 'Shall we have a toast?'

'Sure.' Ryan held up his glass.

'Here's to catching up with old friends.'

'And to new opportunities.' He smiled at her in a way that made her heart squeeze.

'Cheers.' They touched glasses then sipped the wine. 'Mmm. That's a good wine.'

'I like good wine,' Ryan said. 'No point drinking it if it's not delicious. Ready for the movie?'

'Can't wait!'

Carrie settled back against the cushions and the movie began. The fire crackled in the grate, the tree lights flickered, and Ryan was by her side. She was cosy, comfortable and happy. It was so easy being with Ryan, as if they'd never been apart, as if they'd spent their lives together and never lost contact. But in some ways this was even better because despite the years that had passed, they still shared a connection that made her feel all warm inside.

# 10

Carrie walked away from the school dabbing at her eyes. She was just about managing to keep a hold on her emotions.

'That Christmas concert was bloody amazing. Our niece is a star in the making,' Tilly said hooking her arm through Carrie's.

'She is. But then all the children were wonderful.'

'They were. So sweet, innocent and excited about Christmas. They really put their hearts into singing. We were lucky to get tickets for today's matinee, especially seeing as how there are only two performances of it.' Tilly sniffed. 'Do you think Sean will be all right going on his own tomorrow?'

'I'm sure it will be emotional for him. It's such a shame that Lara isn't here to see how wonderful her daughter is.'

'It breaks my heart every time I think

about that.' Tilly sighed. 'I miss her so it must be horrendous for Sean.'

'I know.' Carrie's heart wrenched. 'I wish I could make it all better for him and Gwen.'

'Well I think you make it as good as you can. We're all lucky to have you, Carrie. You're the core of our family.'

'I just love you all and want you to know it.'

'We do, big sister, we do.' Tilly rested her head on Carrie's shoulder. 'Gosh it's cold now.'

Carrie looked up at the leaden sky. The afternoon air felt different too, as if something was coming. Something cold and white, she thought.

'Snow's forecast,' Tilly said as if reading her thoughts.

'Lots of it by the look of the sky.' Carrie shivered.

'You want to come back to mine for a coffee?'

'Thanks, but not today. I need to go for a walk to clear my head after that.'

'A walk, eh? Hoping to wander up to

Shoreview, perhaps?'

'What?' Carrie glanced at her sister as they walked.

'Sean told me all about it. Said that on Saturday you and Ryan looked rather cosy together.'

'We did not. That was five days ago and I haven't seen him since. If we were getting cosy, as you put it, we'd have seen each other this week, wouldn't we?'

'I don't know. You've been working and he probably has too and I know he's had Honey for some playdates with his French bulldog.'

'How do you know all this?'

'Sean, of course.'

'Bloody Sean!'

'It's no wonder Gwen says bloody all the time. She gets it from her loving aunts.'

They both laughed.

When they reached the road that led down to the beach, Tilly stopped walking. 'You sure you don't want to join me? I have that fancy new coffee machine I treated myself to for Christmas.'

'It's not Christmas yet.'

'I know but I couldn't wait to try it.' Tilly grinned. 'And there's no point wrapping it up for myself, is there? I'm hardly going to be surprised when I open it.'

'I guess not.' Carrie shook her head. 'Thanks again but I fancy a walk on the beach.'

'OK, sis. Enjoy and I'll speak to you tomorrow.'

They hugged then Tilly walked away in the direction of the clifftop development.

Carrie wrapped her scarf tighter around her neck and pulled her woolly hat lower over her ears. She hadn't told Tilly that while she had been emotional because the school play was lovely, it was also because she'd been hit by a wave of nostalgia for when Amy had attended the school. Watching her niece dance and sing, Carrie had been taken back to the times she'd watched Amy in school plays, pride making her heart swell. She'd loved those days, had been sure of who she was and what her purpose was: she was a mum, a wife, a daughter, a sister. Her days had been filled with taking care of her family and her home and she'd felt secure of her place in the world. But since Amy had gone off to university, she'd felt a bit adrift. Yes, she had her business, her family and her friends, but Amy no longer needed her in the same way and it took some getting used to.

Down on the sand, she strolled along the shore, swaying as the wind buffeted her. The smell of salt was intense this close to the water and carried by the spray that flew up into the air. Dark brown sand clung to her boots and squelched with each footstep as if trying to hold her in one spot.

When she'd reached the midpoint of the beach, she stopped and stared out to sea. The sky had darkened since they'd left the school but there was a glimmer of brightness on the horizon as if somewhere out there, the sun was breaking through the clouds.

Carrie loved the beach at all times of the year but especially on dramatic winter days like this, when she had it all to herself. Here, as the tide tried to lap at her boots, she felt truly alive and free. And yet today, something lay heavy in her gut like a sandy pebble. She was missing her baby girl and the pain was physical, an ache that made her want to phone Amy immediately to ask her to come home. She'd never do it, of course, knew that Amy had to live her own life, be free to come and go as she pleased. But she missed her and there was no escaping that fact.

She turned at the sound of barking to see Eric and Honey running across the beach. They kept glancing at each other as they ran, then jumping, bowing and running again. Behind them was Ryan, wrapped up in hat, coat and gloves.

When he reached her, his cheeks were rosy and his nose was pink from the chilly air.

'Don't do it,' he said.

'Do what?'

'Go in.' He grimaced. 'It'll be freezing.'

'Oh don't worry. I wasn't going in. I was just breathing in the sea air, taking a moment to clear my head.'

Concern filled his gaze. 'You OK?'

To her dismay, her vision blurred and she raised a hand to wipe her eyes.

'What is it?' He touched her hand and even through their gloves, she felt that spark again.

'Nothing much . . . I'm just missing my girl.'

'Amy?'

She nodded. 'I went to see Gwen's Christmas concert and it was utterly magical but it took me back to when Amy was little. It just hit me how quickly time passes and how much I miss her and . . . the fact that she won't be home for Christmas for the first time ever and I just felt a bit sad.'

'Carrie, that's understandable. It must be hard with her being away and knowing she won't be home this year.'

The kindness in his tone and the

compassion in his gaze proved too much and the hot tears rushed from her eyes and down her cheeks. Before she knew what was happening, strong arms surrounded her and she was swept against a hard chest. For a moment, she didn't respond, and then something in her took over and she wrapped her arms around his waist and hugged him back.

They stayed that way for some time as the waves crashed against the shore, the wind whipped around their legs and the dogs flicked sand around as they chased one another along the beach.

* * *

When Carrie finally pulled gently away and looked up at Ryan, his heart lurched. Her eyes were red and puffy, her nose and chin were red, and her bottom lip was wobbling.

'I know what you need,' he said.

'You do?' She sniffed.

'An alcoholic hot chocolate.'

'That sounds good.'

'It'll warm you up for sure. Why don't you come up to the cottage? I'll light a fire and fix us a drink, wrap you in a blanket and you can tell me all about how you're feeling?'

'Oh my god, Ryan, you don't know how good that sounds.' Her lip wobbled again and he had to fight the urge to try to kiss away her sadness.

'Come on then.'

He wrapped an arm around her shoulders and they crossed the beach and made their way to the cottage. Seeing Carrie so upset had hurt him and he wanted to make her feel better, to be there for her and take care of her.

*Woa! Take care of her?*

Where had that thought come from? Carrie was a strong and independent woman who didn't need taking care of. She was perfectly capable of taking care of herself. But . . . didn't everyone sometimes need a shoulder to cry on? Someone to lean on? A friend to give them a hug and to listen? To Ryan, being there for someone, making them a drink and something to eat, giving them a hug and emotional support was taking care of them.

When they reached the cottage, he unlocked the door then paused. 'I'd probably better get towels for these two before I let them inside. Sandy paws and all that.'

'I'll wait here with them.' Carrie smiled. 'But don't use all your towels because I'd hate to catch you wearing just a hand towel again.'

Ryan laughed. 'That was so embarrassing. It's OK though, I picked up some towels yesterday to use strictly for the dogs. There's no way I'm going to return doggy towels for you to deal with.'

He brought some large colourful towels outside, and while he dried Eric's paws, Carrie dried Honey's. There was something nice about doing this with Carrie, about having company even while completing an ordinary daily task. And the knowledge that she was coming inside with him was like a caffeine buzz fizzing in his veins.

Once the fire was lit, dogs settled on the rug in front of the hearth and drinks made, he sat next to Carrie on the sofa.

'Right then . . . Why don't you tell me what's going on?'

So she did. She told him about how she'd loved being a mum, how fulfilled she'd felt when Amy was a little girl, how she'd hoped to have another baby but it had never happened, about how Amy had suddenly been grown up and gone off to university. Ryan felt like he was watching a movie of her life as she spoke and he admired how openly she described her feelings; how unafraid she was to tell him about her sense of love and loss. Carrie had a big heart and a lot of love to give and he felt sure that when she loved someone, she did it wholeheartedly.

And then it hit him. *Hard.*

He had never fallen in love with a woman since leaving Cwtch Cove and it had been because he'd never stopped loving Carrie. The woman sitting next to him now was the same person he'd cared for growing up, the person he'd wanted to ask out but he'd lost out because Grant had got there first. Once Carrie had given her heart to Grant, she'd have been unable to change that because she was a loyal, loving person. But from what he'd heard since he'd come back to Cwtch Cove, Grant had betrayed that trust, and as far as Ryan was concerned, Grant had lost out.

The question now was . . . Could Carrie love again? Would she be prepared to take a chance on another man? Not just any man, but on Ryan?

He set his mug on the table, feeling the warmth of the brandy in his blood, the heat of something else stirring inside him.

'Carrie?'

Her cheeks were flushed, her hair tousled from her hat and the damp sea breeze. Her pupils dilated as he moved closer on the sofa, making her blue eyes appear darker.

'Yes?'

He took a deep breath then gently

caressed her cheek, ran a finger long her jaw. Her skin was as soft as silk. She gasped with pleasure and tilted her head back so he could run his fingers down her throat and across her collar bones.

'Is this OK?' he asked. 'I . . . I've always liked you, Carrie. I would have asked you out years ago but I couldn't pluck up the courage and when I finally did feel I could do it, Grant asked you first.'

'You always liked me?'

'Of course.'

'I always liked you too.'

'But I was Grant's geeky sidekick. The one with the glasses that were too big for my head and the hair that never looked right in the trendy cuts other boys wore effortlessly.'

'I always thought you were cute and you have gorgeous hair.'

'Cute?'

'Yeah, you know . . . sweet, kind, funny and attractive.'

'I wish I'd known that. I would've asked you out sooner. I thought you were out of my league.'

'Don't be silly. There are no leagues in love and attraction. Would you have kissed me?' She held his gaze and his heart pounded against his rib cage like a trapped bird.

'If you'd wanted me to.' His voice was gruff with desire.

'Well . . . I missed my chance then, but I don't want to miss it again.'

Carrie put her mug down then reached out and slid her arms around his neck. Their eyes locked and as he moved closer to her, need radiated through him. He'd wanted this for so long. Yearned for this for so long. Longed to be with Carrie for what felt like an eternity.

When their lips met, he kissed her softly, felt her breath on his skin, wound his hands through her hair. They explored each other gently at first, but then with more intensity, until the room around them disappeared and they became lost in each other.

# 11

Carrie surveyed the table in her kitchen. There were five places set. There used to be five places when Amy was home but more recently there had been four instead. This evening though, Ryan was joining them for Friday night tacos. Carrie had made a chilli, bought taco shells, nachos and a variety of dips, as well as a few bottles of red wine. She'd also got in some tequila and lime beers and a variety of soft drinks.

She hadn't seen Ryan since the previous morning when she'd woken at his cottage. It had been early, the grey winter light seeping through a gap in the curtains and she'd had to pinch herself to ensure that she wasn't dreaming. One of her first thoughts had been of the cats, but they'd both been in before she'd left the day before and she'd given them their dinner. They had a litter tray in the utility room and a flap in the back door so they could come and go as they pleased. She just hoped they wouldn't have missed her too much.

Ryan had still been asleep so she'd tried to get out of bed quietly, but he had stirred and reached for her. The room had been cold, the bed warm and cosy with their mutual warmth, so she hadn't been keen to leave his arms. They'd hugged for a while and she'd savoured the sensations of being held in strong arms, of skin on skin and the warm morning scent of another human being. A human being she cared deeply about.

But responsibility had called and she had dressed and left, knowing she couldn't be late for work and that she had to feed the cats. She'd felt a bit strange; it had been a long time since she'd spent the night with anyone and it had been wonderful but also kind of unsettling. She liked Ryan a lot, felt more than like for him, but she wasn't sure where it could go. If it would go anywhere. Ryan had said lovely things to her but wasn't that what men did? Said things to woo you, lived with you and made a family with you then one day, broke your heart?

*But this is Ryan! He's different . . .*

A voice in her mind kept repeating this and she wanted to believe it, but she was scared. And so, she'd stayed home alone last night to have some time to think. Part of her had longed to go to Ryan, to fall into his arms and make love again but the other part had told her to stay cool and calm. She was forty-five, had responsibilities and couldn't afford to behave recklessly. Even if she wanted to believe that Ryan's intentions were good.

Was it really Ryan she doubted or was it herself? Her ability to commit to another man and relationship after what had happened with Grant? She'd given herself to Grant in every way, had trusted him with her body, heart and mind and even though there had been bumps in the road over the years, she'd thought what they had was solid enough to last the distance. But it hadn't been enough for Grant; *she* hadn't been enough for Grant.

What if she wasn't enough for Ryan? Could she take that chance? She'd rebuilt her life once but she didn't know if she could do it again. Sean and Gwen needed her. Tilly needed her. Amy, in her own way, needed her.

Dinner this evening had seemed like a good step to take. Ryan could spend some time with her family and she could see how he interacted with them, find out what they thought about him. It was a safe way to spend time with him that wouldn't involve taking their clothes off because she knew if that happened again, she'd throw caution to the wind. How had she forgotten what desire felt like? How had she lived without passion all this time?

'Evening!' Tilly called from the hallway, making Carrie shake herself to clear the thoughts of Ryan away. 'Only me.'

'I'm in the kitchen.'

'I know! I could smell the chilli from out on the street.'

Carrie laughed. 'I hope that's a good thing.'

'Definitely.' Tilly sashayed into the kitchen in a cloud of fresh air and expensive perfume. She placed a bag on the table then hugged Carrie. 'And I am ravenous!'

'I'm glad to hear it. There's plenty here so you can have second helpings and even take some home for your freezer.'

'I love it when you look after me!' Tilly grinned. 'Right . . . what can I do to help?'

'Open some wine?'

'Brilliant!' Tilly opened a bottle of red then poured some into two glasses and handed one to Carrie. 'Cheers!'

'Cheers.'

'This is delicious.'

'I know. I got the recommendation from Ryan.'

'Did you now?' Tilly raised her eyebrows. 'And how's that going?'

'How's what going?'

'Oh come on, Carrie, pull the other one and it'll play *Jingle Bells*.'

'What?' Carrie snorted.

'You know what I mean. You and

Ryan . . . Is it official now?'

'Just because I invited him for dinner?'

'I heard . . . from a source . . . that your van was parked outside Shore House Cottage all night on Wednesday.'

Carrie turned to the stove and stirred the chilli, watching the ground beef, mixed beans and tomatoes simmer in their rich sauce. That hadn't been something she'd wanted to share with her sister or with anyone at this point; she'd intended on keeping it to herself. But in a small village, privacy wasn't always possible. She should have been more careful. What if Amy found out?

'What source told you that?'

'One of the vet nurses was walking her dog early and she saw your van there. You can hardly miss it with Dust Busters in bold on the side. Even from down on the beach.'

'Great.' Carrie rubbed her eyes. 'So now I'm the centre of village gossip, am I?'

'Not at all.' Tilly came to Carrie and hugged her from behind. 'Don't be so hard on yourself. It was a passing comment and I just told her that you couldn't start the van after you'd been cleaning up there, so you had a lift home with Sean. I then told Sean to back me up if anyone asked him.'

'You told Sean?' Carrie turned in Tilly's embrace and sighed. 'So now my brother and my sister both think I'm sleeping around.'

'Hardly!' Tilly waved a hand dismissively. 'Carrie, you've been single now for what . . . fifteen years? That's a long time. You're an amazing person and you have every right to enjoy yourself. Ryan seems nice and Sean approves of him. In fact, Sean said he thinks Ryan is a great guy.'

'What is this? Regency England? Are you and Sean playing matchmakers? How much have you set aside for my dowry?'

'Carrie!' Tilly picked up her glass and sipped her wine. 'Chill out! I'm teasing you. But . . . I'm also telling you that it's OK for you to have sex. It's OK for you to have fun. It's OK for you to fall in love . . . if that's what's happening here. And don't worry about who knows it. You're entitled to live your life for you. I think you forget that sometimes.'

'Look . . . I like Ryan. He is very nice and he's handsome and yes, we did spend the night together.' Her cheeks flooded with heat as she said the words out loud. 'I'm a bit embarrassed about it but it was also . . . lovely.'

'Don't be embarrassed! And I'm delighted it was lovely. You should be having plenty of sex. It's good for you.'

'What, like you are?' Carrie winced as the words tripped off her tongue and she saw the wounded expression on Tilly's face. 'Oh, love, I'm sorry. I didn't mean to say that.'

Tilly shrugged. 'It's fine. And you're right; I am a hypocrite. But I just can't seem to find the energy or the inclination to start dating again.'

'It will come.' Carrie squeezed Tilly's shoulder. 'When you're ready and the right person comes along.'

'Maybe. But for now, I'm happy as I am and over the moon that my big sister is seeing someone.'

'We're not exactly seeing each other though. We've *seen* each other a few times and we spent one night together but that's it.'

'But he's coming for dinner?'

'Yes.'

'And he might stay the night?'

'Absolutely not.' Carrie shook her head. 'The only warm bodies in my bed tonight will be my own and the cats.'

'We'll see.' Tilly laughed. 'We'll see.'

'Aunty Carrie! We're here.' Gwen called from the front door.

'In the kitchen!' Carrie replied loudly, then she whispered, 'Now shush about it, Tilly. The last thing I want is Gwen asking about my sex life.'

'My lips are sealed.' Tilly closed her mouth and pretended to zip it up.

'Glad to hear it.' Carrie winked at her then turned to Gwen as she hurtled into the kitchen.

* * *

Ryan looked up as footsteps thudded overhead. 'Do you think they're all right up there?' he asked.

'I'll go and check.' Sean stood up. 'Just in case poor Eric has been tucked into bed or locked in a wardrobe.'

What?' Ryan pushed his chair back, concern about his dog rushing through him. 'I don't think he'll be happy about that.'

'I'm joking.' Sean held up a hand. 'Gwen wouldn't lock him in a wardrobe, but she might have tucked him into bed. It happens sometimes with the cats. Well, with Purrito anyway. Mittens won't allow it.'

'OK.' Ryan tucked his chair in again and reached for his wine glass. Honey was at his side, where she'd been through dinner, waiting patiently for someone to offer her a tasty morsel from the table. Ryan had sneaked her a few nachos with melted cheese on and she'd remained next to him as his faithful companion.

She'd stayed with him and Eric for the previous two nights and the dogs were getting on well. He'd decided he'd definitely adopt her and Sean was delighted. Unlike Eric though, who'd happily gone upstairs to play with Gwen after dinner, Honey had stuck by Ryan. He thought it was mainly because of the food but liked to think it might also be because she was growing fond of him.

'More wine, Ryan?' Tilly asked.

'Yes please.' He held out his glass and she filled it.

'Carrie?'

'Go on then.' Carrie was sitting opposite Ryan at the table and had been very busy all evening. Her family had already been here when he'd arrived so he hadn't had a chance to speak to her alone and she'd seemed to be avoiding eye contact with him. He was finding it tough because all he wanted was to give her a hug and ask how she felt about the night they'd spent together. She looked beautiful this evening with her blonde bob clipped back, wearing a pale blue shirt that made her eyes seem brighter than usual and baggy jeans that were rolled up at the ankles. She had a pair of novelty reindeer slippers on that she said Amy had given her last year. Ryan knew that Eric had eyed them up over the course of the evening and suspected that if Carrie removed them at any point, Eric would run off with one.

But even in everyday clothes, Carrie looked amazing. She always had. And her curves that had developed as she'd got older, that he'd seen without clothing . . .

He shook himself inwardly. Thinking about her shape, her soft skin and how she felt in his arms was not appropriate right now. He hoped he'd get to hold her later because he didn't know how he'd cope if he had to leave without so much as a hug. He'd missed her last night but had understood when she'd texted him to say that she was tired and needed a good sleep. He was tired too; a night of passion would do that to you, whatever age you were. Some space was probably a good thing, even if the bed had felt empty without her in his arms.

'Are you going to keep lovely Honey then?' Tilly asked, snapping him from his thoughts.

'I hope so, yes. She's gentle and sweet and Eric adores her. As do I,' he said, smiling at Tilly. She was a lot like Carrie with the same shaped face, blue eyes and blonde hair — although hers was cropped short — but she was very thin and there was something haunted about her eyes that suggested she'd been through a tough time. When he'd left Cwtch Cove for university, Tilly had been a little girl, Carrie's younger sister, so he hadn't really known her very well. Now, she was a lawyer with a fancy house on the clifftop. She'd been very friendly this evening though and he wondered how much she knew about him and Carrie. Did she have any suspicions and what would she think if she did? Would she approve of him? He really hoped so because he knew how important family was to Carrie.

'Right, I'll clear the table and wash up then we can have some dessert.' Carrie stood up.

'I'll do it!' Ryan pushed his chair back carefully so Honey wouldn't be startled.

'It's fine, you're a guest.' Carrie shook her head.

'And you cooked a wonderful meal, so you must sit down and enjoy your wine while I do the dishes.' Ryan started to gather plates from the table.

'How about we do it together?' Carrie said. 'There's quite a lot here.'

'I'll just pop and check on Gwen and Sean.' Tilly flashed a knowing smile at them both before leaving the room.

'Are you OK?' Ryan asked, not knowing how long they'd have alone.

Carrie nodded. 'I'm OK. Are you?'

'As long as you are.'

Carrie put the plates she was holding on the worktop then took his hand. 'Thanks for coming.'

'Thanks for inviting me.' He smiled at her shyly, feeling like an awkward teenager, so when Carrie moved to her tiptoes and pressed a gentle kiss to his lips, relief rushed through him. He pulled her into a hug and kissed the top of her hair that smelt of apple shampoo and spices from the chilli. 'I've been wanting to do this all evening,' he said.

'Me too,' she replied, hugging him tighter.

* * *

The next morning, Ryan woke to find Carrie sitting up on the bed next to him, staring at the wall. She was outside of the duvet, wearing an oversized jumper and thick socks. Her hair was tousled from the night before and it made him smile.

'Morning,' he said, sitting up and taking her hand.

She blinked then turned to look at him. 'Hi.'

'How did you sleep?'

'All right, thanks. Until around four-thirty when I heard the dogs walking around downstairs.'

Eric and Honey had been given the

lounge to sleep in and when Ryan and Carrie had come upstairs, Purrito had been snuggling against Honey and purring loudly. Mittens, though, had let herself out through the cat flap, clearly disapproving of their overnight guests. Carrie had told Ryan not to worry about Mittens as she'd come home when she was ready and probably head upstairs to Amy's room.

'Sorry. I must've slept right through.' He rubbed his eyes. After making love to Carrie, he'd fallen asleep with her wrapped in his arms and clearly been out cold all night. 'I was extremely relaxed.'

Carrie's lips curved upwards slightly then her mouth tightened into a thin line as if she was gritting her teeth together.

'What's wrong?' he asked, a sinking feeling trickling through him.

She sighed and picked at a cuticle. 'I'm just a bit tired, I think. I have to work this morning too.'

'On a Saturday?'

'Yes. I have to . . . sort through the van and see what products I need to order in.'

‘I could help with that?’ He turned to face her, worry gnawing at his edges.

‘No, thanks. It’s fine. I’d prefer to do it alone. Not much room in there, you know.’

‘OK,’ he said. ‘I should probably get the dogs back to the cottage, anyway.’

She nodded and his heart sank. He’d been hoping she’d insist he stay for breakfast or even just coffee. Talk to him at least.

‘I guess so,’ she said, sliding off the bed and going to the door. ‘I’m going to shower and brush my teeth.’

When she’d gone, Ryan pulled his knees up to his chest and rested his elbows on them. What had happened between now and last night to change everything? They’d had a wonderful evening with Carrie’s family, had eaten, drunk wine and played some games with Gwen. They’d laughed a lot. They’d shared a hug and kiss in the kitchen and Carrie had seemed to want to be close to Ryan. After everyone had gone, they’d fallen into bed together and made slow, sensual love. Twice. And now . . . it seemed that she wanted him gone as quickly as possible.

Hurt and sadness enveloped him like a black cloud as he got up and dressed then padded down the stairs. He didn't know what had changed for Carrie but he didn't want to crowd her. She clearly needed space and so that was what he'd give her. Caring for people was scary; it came with risks. You had to make yourself vulnerable to love someone and perhaps Carrie wasn't in the right place to do that. Ryan truly believed that he was in the right place and he hoped Carrie would find it in her heart to give him a chance, but if she couldn't, then he had no choice other than to accept that.

'Hey guys,' he said, when he found Eric and Honey in the lounge doorway wagging their tails. At least they were happy to see him this morning. 'We'd better head on home and get your breakfast ready.'

He pulled on his coat and hat, fastened the dogs' harnesses and leads on over their coats then went to the bottom of the stairs.

'I'm going now, Carrie. I'll text you later, shall I?'

There was no reply, only the faint sound of running water from the bathroom, and in his ears, the thudding of his broken heart.

# 12

'Slow down, Carrie! It's too early on a Monday morning to expend so much energy.'

She looked up to find Levi staring at her in the mirror. They were cleaning a holiday cottage that would be occupied by guests over Christmas. It was on the same site as Ryan's and Carrie had been worried about catching sight of him all morning. She'd driven there taking the long way around to avoid passing Shore House but even so, she could still see his car from the front window of the cottage and it made her feel shaky.

Since Saturday, she'd felt physically ill. She'd basically pushed Ryan out the door in the morning and guilt was churning in her gut. But she also felt incredibly sad, like she'd lost something precious, and in a way she had. Ryan was a friend and had been one for a long time and when their friendship had become something more, she'd turned on him, let him down. That was the last thing she'd wanted to do but after they'd spent another night together, she'd woken up terrified.

She sprayed more cleaner on the sink and scrubbed harder.

'Carrie!' Levi touched her shoulder. 'Please slow down. You'll wear the sink away at this rate.'

Daisy entered the small bathroom. 'He's right, Carrie. You've been like a spinning top this morning and Levi and I are worried about you. Come and have a cuppa and tell us what's going on.'

Carrie looked at her reflection. Her hair was tied back with a scarf and her face was pale, her eyes red rimmed with dark purple shadows beneath them. She didn't look well so it was no wonder that her employees, who were also her friends and who she spent a lot of time with, were worried. She'd be the same if one of them was behaving in this way and looked this poorly.

She sagged against the sink. Levi took

the sponge and spray from her hands, peeled her yellow rubber gloves off then led her down the stairs and into the kitchen. He made her sit at the table while Daisy made them all a cup of tea.

'Now then, Carrie, want to tell us what's going on? We might be able to help,' Daisy said.

'I've done a silly thing,' she said.

'Does it have anything to do with that hot guy who's been in the village? Whose parents' house we cleaned?' Levi asked.

'Yes, the one who's renting Shore House?' Daisy nodded. 'Ryan, isn't it?'

'Yes.' Carrie sighed, covering her face with her hands. 'I spent the night with him.'

'Woo hoo!' Levi clapped his hands. 'That's amazing!'

'Twice.' Carrie blushed as she lowered her hands.

'Good on you, girl!' Daisy patted her hand. 'We wondered if you'd ever get back on the bicycle.'

Carrie said, 'I really like him. He's always been a friend . . . we grew up together, in fact. He's kind and caring and he said he really likes me. Has always liked me. I feel a bit silly saying this because I'm fifty in five years' time. I'm not a teenager, not even a twenty-something like you, Levi. I should be past all this. Shouldn't I?'

'Why?' Levi shook his head. 'You're a gorgeous woman who has every right to want some love and romance in your life. As well as some hanky-panky.'

'Hanky-panky?' Daisy sniggered. 'More like horizontal hokey-pokey.'

'Or no-pants dance.' Levi shimmied on the chair as if showing off his dance moves.

'Cut it out you two!' Carrie shook her head. 'This is exactly why I didn't want to tell you.'

'We're teasing you, Carrie!' Daisy tapped her hand on the table and the tea sloshed in the mugs. 'You're both gorgeous adults and the two of you are well matched. Enjoy it!'

'What if it . . . whatever *it* is, doesn't work out?' Carrie asked.

'What if it doesn't?' Daisy cocked an eyebrow. 'You'll have had a nice festive fling and life will go on.'

'Darling Carrie,' Levi said like he was twenty years older than her and not the other way around, 'You only regret the chances you don't take.'

Carrie smiled. 'I know you're right but I'm scared.'

'It's OK to be scared. Feel the feeling and do it anyway. If you don't try, you'll never know, will you?' Daisy asked.

'That's true.' Carrie nodded.

A knock at the door made them all freeze.

'Who's that?' Levi said, standing up.

'Hold on, I'll just use my magical powers.' Daisy scrunched up her face and placed two fingers on either side of her head.

'Shut up you moron!' Levi flounced out of the kitchen.

Carrie heard the door opening and Levi greeting someone then he returned to the kitchen, cheeks flushed and eyes wide. 'Carrie, there's someone here to speak to you.'

'Oh.' She stood up.

'Go on, now! Take a chance,' Levi whispered as he ushered her out to the hallway then closed the kitchen door.

There, standing in the open doorway, was Ryan.

'I'm sorry,' he said. 'I know I should stay away and give you space but I just . . . I felt so . . .' His eyes shone behind his glasses so he rubbed at them with his fingertips. 'If I've messed up, I'm so sorry. I really am. Please can we still be friends, even if you don't want anything else from me?'

Carrie gazed into his eyes. There was nothing there other than genuine emotion. He was still the Ryan she'd always known. One of the good guys.

'I'm so sorry,' she said. 'I've been an idiot. I'm just terrified of getting hurt again so I panicked and shut down. Or tried to, because I feel ill, so I clearly didn't do a very good job of it. After we spent the night together the first time I felt anxious, but the second time, I just knew . . .' She gnawed at her bottom lip.

'You knew what?' he asked, fear in his eyes.

'That I care for you deeply. That I always have. It wasn't just nostalgia or fleeting attraction . . . It's so much more.'

He nodded and raised his hands but paused as if uncertain. Carrie took hold of them and brought them to her chest and squeezed them tight.

'Since Grant left, I've been focused on being a mum, on my business, on supporting my brother and sister. I thought I'd closed myself off to romance and to any notions of romantic involvement but clearly, I was wrong. However, I couldn't fall for just anyone.'

'No?' his voice wavered.

'No, Ryan . . . It had to be you.'

A tear trickled down his cheek, so she brushed it away with her lips, then she let go of his hands and wound her arms around his neck. 'I can't deny that I'm scared though, Ryan.'

'Me too, Carrie. But I promise I'll never hurt you. I'm not like Grant at all.'

'You never were.'

'So what do we do?' he asked, resting his hands gently on her waist.

'I think . . . We take a chance.'

'Are you sure?'

'I'm sure because this would be a chance I'd regret not taking.'

She moved closer and kissed him, felt him relax in her embrace, and as the snow began to fall outside, all her fears and worries melted away.

# Epilogue

'Ta da!' Carrie set the turkey on the table then stood back.

'It all looks bloody amazing, Aunty Carrie,' Gwen said.

'Ryan helped.' Carrie smiled at Ryan as he put a large dish of roast potatoes next to the turkey. 'He even made cranberry sauce.'

'I'd say he's a keeper,' Tilly muttered with a wink and Carrie laughed.

In the six days since Ryan had come to speak to her, they'd tried to take things slowly but it was proving impossible because they couldn't keep their hands off each other. It was like they were making up for lost time, for all those years when they could have been together if things had happened differently. Carrie didn't wish that they had though because she wouldn't have had Amy then, plus there was something nice about having the opportunity to fall in love in her forties. She was convinced that she was falling in love, that the seeds of her feelings had been planted long ago but they'd lain dormant like spring bulbs and now, years later, they were poking their shoots above the soil.

They were also in a different place than they'd have been in their teens and twenties. They had secure incomes, Carrie owned her home, she had an adult daughter and two cats. Ryan had two dogs and from what he'd told her, substantial savings. There was no rush, no pressure and they could enjoy spending time together and getting to know each other properly all over again.

The fact that Ryan had been up since six helping her prepare Christmas dinner for her family had made her heart squeeze. Grant had never helped, not once, but from what she'd seen so far, Ryan was amazing in the kitchen and saw their relationship as a partnership. They hadn't discussed moving in together yet, had agreed to enjoy their time and to see how things went after Christmas, but Carrie couldn't imagine not wanting him around now. She knew she could never leave Cwtch Cove and Ryan had told her that he missed his parents and wanted to spend more time with them, so it looked as though he might move back home.

She sat down and accepted a glass of champagne from Tilly then held it up. 'Here's to a magical Christmas,' she said. 'Cheers Ryan, Tilly, Gwen, Sean, Griffin and Blodwen.'

'Cheers!' they all replied.

Next to the table, Eric and Honey sat in their new large bed that Ryan had bought so they could share it, watching everyone, keen to pounce on anything that might fall to the floor. Purrito and Mittens waited near the back door, the picture of feline nonchalance, confident that Carrie would give them their share of turkey once dinner was done.

She sipped her champagne, enjoying the cool crisp taste, the fizz of the bubbles against her tongue and smiled, as under the table, Ryan took hold of her hand.

‘Merry Christmas,’ he said, giving her fingers a squeeze.

‘Merry Christmas, my love,’ she replied.

And Carrie knew that she’d been right to take a chance this Christmas at Cwtch Cove.

*Other titles in the Linford Romance Library:*

## CHRISTMAS CAKE CHATEAU

**De-ann Black**

Colouring book artist Lucy has booked a stay at a beautiful little cottage on the estate of a magnificent chateau in Scotland, intending to get away from the city to finish her latest book. But there is filming going on at the chateau, and this messes up her plans for a quiet working holiday.

Struan is the handsome owner of the hotel, known as the Christmas Cake Chateau, and involves Lucy in the light-hearted chaos. Lucy just wants to work on her floral illustrations — but Struan and others become a tempting distraction . . .

## AN OUTBACK CHRISTMAS

### Alan C. Williams

A dream trip to Australia goes horribly wrong for Jill when her boyfriend empties their joint account and disappears, leaving her high and dry. But a change of luck leads her to a job as a jillaroo on a sheep station, to new friends, a new lifestyle, and possibly a new love . . .

# CHRISTMAS WITH CARY

## Sharon Booth

Molly's spent every Christmas she can remember surrounded by her family. But this year is different. She's all alone in a strange town. She's left her family behind, and she's not sure where she can call home any longer. All Molly has with her are a few clothes in a suitcase, and a collection of her old friend's Cary Grant films.

Except there's one more thing she's brought along — the whole reason for her Christmas visit. In her possession is a small, crumpled piece of paper, and on it is written the address of the love of her life . . .